AN AMERICAN CONSPIRACY

A Novel

ALAN C. MOORE

FREILING
PUBLISHING

Published by Freiling Publishing,
a division of Freiling Agency, LLC.

P.O. Box 1264
Warrenton, VA 20188

www.FreilingPublishing.com

PB ISBN: 978-1-956267-42-6
eBook ISBN: 978-1-956267-43-3

Printed in the United States of America

For Kristin, Shannon, Patrick,
and the rest of my loving family.

CHAPTER 1

THE MORNING PRAYERS DID LITTLE TO comfort Yasin for his death.

Riyadh was hot and dry as it is every day, but the heat was not causing Yasin to sweat. The growing fear inside of him could not be ignored as the suicide vest under his thawb grew as heavy as his anxiety.

Yasin removed his cell phone with shaking hands. He walked toward the skyscraper and dialed the memorized number. He was a few blocks away from the target.

"Yes?" A gruff voice answered.

"Hello, I, uh, am having difficulties," Yasin responded.

"What is wrong?"

"I'm scared."

The man replied in a cold but empathetic voice, "That is natural for a teenager but you must remember you are doing the work of Allah. Remember the Quran reads, *'Fighting is prescribed for you, and ye dislike it. But it is possible that ye dislike a thing which is good for you, and that ye love a thing which is bad for you. But Allah knoweth, and ye know not.'*"

Yasin stopped at the main entrance of the Kingdom Centre Mall. He stared in awe at the immense forty-one-story skyscraper.

"Are you there yet?" The man asked.

"Yes," Yasin replied.

"Look at this symbol of apostasy. Greed oozes from the opulence of this sinful landmark."

Yasin watched as guards patted down single males entering the mall. Others were waiting to pass through metal detectors.

He breathed deeply and nodded.

"Yes, you are right, brother," Yasin said. "What must I do? The security is tight."

"Ok, fine. Walk to the right and make your way to the back of the building. You will see an emergency exit. The door will be propped open. Enter quickly and quietly."

Yasin found the door with ease. A small piece of paper wedged it open. He entered what appeared to be a storeroom, with *Cartier* emblazoned on various boxes. Finding himself alone, he slipped into the front of the store then onto the main causeway.

"I'm inside."

"Good, now make your way to the food court."

The mall was packed with hundreds of women in black burqas. Men strode, shopping bags in hand, with their families. Children, some as small as toddlers, happily accompanied their parents.

There were easily 1,000 people in the food court. Yasin sat at an unoccupied table and watched oblivious bystanders. He felt invisible.

"Now," the man said, "I'll walk you through this. Wait until I give the order."

Yasin sweated even more. Stress mounted as he reached under his thawb for the detonator. He was trained well yet he could not shake a nagging feeling. He fingered the trigger but not enough to risk a premature explosion.

"Soon, my brother," the man said in a soothing tone.

"What is taking so long?" Yasin snapped.

"Calm down. There is a certain special individual who is visiting the food court today. I'm waiting for confirmation of his arrival."

"Who?"

"Does it matter?"

"Maybe, perhaps... yes, it does."

"I cannot tell you, but rest assured, this person's death will strike fear into the hearts of infidels who have corrupted the government. When he dies, you will be hailed as a victor. Your place in *Jannah* will be assured as you rest in eternal peace with all the pious martyrs."

Yasin's thoughts quickly raced toward the harshest of realities. In his mind, he saw bodies strewn across the mall. Men, women, and children were disembodied and obliterated by the blast.

"Surely, there are true warriors of God in here today, are there not?" Yasin whispered into the phone.

The man at the end of the line hesitated then said, "I know you are tense, brother. But listen to me. You must not fret. Your time for martyrdom is at hand."

"It is still my choice. I owe you nothing. Again, are there not true followers of Allah here today? How do you know they all deserve this fate?"

"There are always casualties in war. Allah accepts this because our cause is holy. You will be rewarded."

"Will I?" Yasin raised his voice. A few men sitting at a nearby table glanced in his direction.

"Quiet! Calm yourself. Do not spend your last few minutes in such an undignified manner. You..."

Yasin put the phone down. He barely heard the man's muffled words. He took a deep breath then put the phone back to his ear.

"Surely Allah has more plans for me than this?"

"There is no greater honor. You are lucky to have been chosen for such a holy task. Look... wait."

The line went silent for a moment.

"Ok, listen, Yasin, I have the confirmation I needed. The time is now. Take your rightful place among the martyrs. Muhammad awaits you in paradise. Go, now, press the button!"

Yasin began to cry.

He removed his finger from the trigger and stood facing the nearest exit.

"No," he said. "May Allah forgive my weakness. But I will not commit murder in His name today."

"Yasin." The voice on the other end of the line turned grim.

"Do not bother convincing me, it is settled."

"You are exactly what I thought you were," the man said. "And by the way... there is *no* Allah."

The last noise Yasin heard was the beep of the suicide vest as it received the radio signal from the man on the phone.

The explosion was nothing short of catastrophic.

It would take days before the death toll was fully confirmed.

CHAPTER 2

THE OPULENCE OF THEIR SURROUNDINGS COULD not drown out the sullen mood of the conversation. Madison gaped at her mentor as he shuffled his chicken biryani with his fork. The Bombay Club was bustling during the lunch hour. Some of the most powerful people in Washington, D.C., were hobnobbing at tables around the two legislators as their conversation had reached levels on the apex of bizarre.

"Paging Senator Radford," Madison said.

Boyd glanced up and cracked a smile. "Madison, you know better than to call me that."

"Of course I do. But it's the only thing I could do to get your attention. You are never this distracted, what's up?"

Senator Boyd Radford put down his fork and crossed his hands over his lap. "Tell me, how would you rate your first six months in office?" he asked.

"Honestly? Uneventful. No one seems particularly interested in anything I've tried to do thus far, which admittedly, is very little."

Boyd smiled. "That will come with time. You're new. No one gets anything done their first few terms in the House."

"About that," she jumped in, "I wanted to talk to you about some energy reform policies…"

Her voice trailed off as the senator went numb again and gazed into nowhere.

"You know," he spoke as if to no one in particular, "Can you believe that I have seven grandkids? Twenty years in public life and that is my proudest accomplishment. God, I love those kids. So beautiful, so innocent."

Madison hoped the twitch in her eye did not reveal her annoyance. "I thought we were here to work. If not, that's fine. I just want to stay on track."

"Work, work, work," he said playfully. "You are a fine congresswoman and an even better person. Do not let this cesspool of a town bring you down."

"I don't think I could. It's too ingrained in me I'm afraid." Madison remembered the moment she decided to run for Congress. She was having a quiet drink with her husband, John. Madison was bored with her life. She had run from her political upbringing for too long and yet John realized it before Madison. If it were not for his insistence and support, Madison never would have made the jump to politics.

It was an ominous task. For a woman with no experience holding office, running for Congress was daunting. Madison was well aware that her last name would give her an undeserved boost. If it had been up to her, she would have taken that aspect out of the equation. Either way, it was risky to move back from New York with the sole intention of launching a congressional campaign. The voters could have rejected Madison for any number of fairly legitimate reasons.

But never did fear come into play. Madison decided if she lost the election then it was never meant to be. She would move on to other things. Her personal life had been the subject of public scrutiny for as long as she could remember. There was no risk of airing dirty laundry because, truthfully, there was little there. She kept her nose clean her whole life. Anything her political opposition threw at her she took in stride. And that is an essential trait for any successful politician.

Senator Radford hesitated then shuddered, asking, "Do you speak with William much these days?"

Madison frowned. "Eh. Things between us have been better."

"I know he's your father, but he's a real son of a bitch."

Madison failed to hide the shock on her face. She had the same thoughts about William many times. But to hear it from someone like her mentor caught her off guard. "So you've closed the doors on reconciling, being friends again?"

"Well, no one really has friends in this city," he sighed. "He wasn't much of an ally to you during your campaign. That annoyed me."

"But it wasn't unexpected," Madison said. She shoved her plate away.

Boyd nodded. "How's his health?"

Madison went stone-faced, "I really couldn't say."

"Ah, I see."

"You haven't asked about my father in some time. You're acting strange today."

Boyd sipped his water, wiped his mouth, and gazed at Madison with solemnity. "Maddy, this city is awful, and you know better than most. You remind me so much of me when I first came to Congress. You're not the idealistic 'Mrs. Smith goes to Washington' and I love that about you. You're a pragmatist and most politicians don't get that way for at least a few years of office under their belt."

"I'm just trying to do the best I can." Madison hated praise. "Boyd, seriously, what's wrong? Enough with the games."

The senator smiled. "You've got great instincts, my dear, but you don't know everything. Some things are going to happen very soon. I wish I could elaborate but you have to trust me. It will be very difficult for you to understand and you will want answers. I won't be able to give them to you. Just keep your nose clean. My God, just stay out of trouble."

"I need more than that." Madison said. She crossed her arms and leaned back. The waiter dropped off the bill but before he said anything Madison waved him away.

Boyd scanned the room. "Secrets are the fuel that keeps this city burning," he whispered. "I thought I could play the game better than anyone…but I was wrong. You are bound to have things happen that you don't want the public to discover, but do try to limit such things."

Madison put her hand on top of Boyd's. "Is someone blackmailing you?"

"No, not me," he said quickly, still scanning the room.

"Then who?"

"Everyone else," he replied under his breath.

Madison sat back. "You're scaring me," she said.

"No, I'm not. Nothing scares you. Forgive me, Maddy. I should not speak like this; I really don't want you to worry. Everything will be fine. I have to take care of something back in my office then it will be finished. Please, trust me. The melodramatics comes with old age. It really is nothing more than that. I have to get to work, I'm sorry."

Boyd and Madison stood. Her perplexed look subsided as he put his arm around her back like a father to a daughter. It was reminiscent of old times before the drama of politics took a foothold in both their lives.

Madison was not a block toward her office when her phone buzzed. "I've got to take this call. I'll take it walking back if you don't mind."

Senator Radford nodded then watched her leave as he hailed a cab. At his age he didn't have the stamina for a two-mile walk like the younger and more athletic Madison. As a taxi pulled up, he thought how enjoyable it was to smash his cell phone earlier in the day. Boyd was so close to freedom.

The senator told the driver, "Hart Senate Office Building."

The cabbie grunted and drove off.

A few minutes later, Boyd was staring at his office computer screen. He opened a drawer in his desk, reached for a bottle of Wasmund's Single Malt, and poured a generous glass. He took two large gulps, rubbed his temples, and gazed at the picture of his wife on the desk.

He typed a few words on his computer then turned off the monitor.

Boyd opened another drawer and removed a loaded Smith & Wesson Centerfire Revolver.

"God, forgive me," he said as he placed the gun in his mouth.

He took a deep breath and closed his eyes.

Then, he pulled the trigger.

CHAPTER 3

MADISON GLARED OUT THE WINDOW OF her tiny office with a vacant expression. First-term representatives always received the worst pick in the office lottery. The view was uninspiring, just office windows and a few air conditioning units along an empty walkway. Until this point, she did not mind, in fact, this was the first time she ever spent any brain matter thinking about the view. Her eyes were almost always glued to whatever piece of business was up next in her busy schedule. Now though, she appreciated the distraction from the FBI agent in the room.

"I understand you were close with the deceased?" the agent asked.

Madison heard the question, but it sounded distant like someone was speaking in mumbles or underwater. She did not respond, waiting for the agent to ask her again. But he waited politely. Madison turned and tried to smile, but failed. She blinked and said, "Boyd and I were very close. He was like a father to me."

"I understand."

"Do you?" Madison snapped.

The agent froze.

Madison shook her head. Tears rolled down. "As you can tell, I'm a little on edge right now," she admitted.

"I wouldn't expect anything less. And I realize this is difficult." The agent scribbled in a notebook.

"I just had lunch with the man. I never thought he would ever do something like this."

"That's why I wanted to just clear some things up. That lunch in particular, I was wondering—"

Madison interrupted, "What was your name again?"

"Special Agent Walter Robinson, ma'am."

"You can drop that ma'am stuff and tell me why he took his life?"

Agent Robinson turned his attention away from his notebook. "That's what I'm trying to find out. What did you discuss at lunch?"

"Nothing really. Boyd seemed distracted but calm. It was out of the ordinary, I'll admit, but he did not seem overly stressed."

"Did he say anything unusual?"

Madison wondered if the agent noticed the redness in her eyes. She suddenly remembered the speech Boyd had given at her wedding. He spoke of toughness and never taking the easy way out in politics or marriage. It tore Madison to believe her mentor was so distressed that he could not face the problem. Boyd survived so many attacks from enemies in the past. What could have been so terrible for him to take his own life? "Well, he was coy. There was something on his mind. He said one peculiar thing."

"Which was?"

"Secrets are the fuel that keeps this city burning."

Agent Robinson raised his left eyebrow. "Really? What was that in reference to?"

"He wouldn't elaborate. I'm afraid that's really all I know."

Walter scribbled in his notebook again. He twisted his lips and tapped his pen on his cheek.

"What is it? And why is the FBI investigating a suicide? I thought the Capitol Police would have jurisdiction over this before calling you in, no?" Madison did not know why she was being so evasive with this FBI agent. The anger inside boiled over.

"Well, I probably shouldn't say, but, I am trying to find signs of blackmail."

Madison slammed her fist on the desk. The air in the office suddenly seemed more stuffy than usual. "You think someone was trying to get something out of him? For what?"

Walter took a step back as if Madison was about to combust into an anger-fueled burst of flames. "I don't think anything of the sort, yet."

"But you're going to find out?"

"I hope so."

This was becoming infuriating. "Did he leave a suicide note? He must have."

"I can't say."

"You don't know, or you can't say?"

"Pick one."

Madison leered at Agent Robinson as if he had just confessed to murder. Walter used his best poker face, but on the inside, he thought how glad he was to be armed.

A knock at the door momentarily cut the tension. Madison's chief of staff, Jason Phillips, entered the room. Madison did little to hide her annoyance.

"Jason, what is it?" she bellowed.

"I'm sorry, Congresswoman, but I have something important."

Madison loudly tapped her fingers on her desk.

"Right," Jason said, calling himself to attention. "I have a producer on the line from the *Newscycle* with Reginald Goldsmith. They want to talk about Senator Radford since they knew you two were close. Reginald has a five minute time slot available tonight. They could send a car to take you to their local affiliate so you could do the interview over satellite with him in New York. But you would have to leave soon. I know you're busy right now but this couldn't wait."

"Yes it could!" Madison yelled. "Are you seriously asking me to do a television spot to talk about my friend and mentor who just *killed* himself?"

Jason froze. He waited for the tongue lashing to continue before attempting to sheepishly withdraw. She twitched her face as if to say, "Well?"

"I… uh… normally wouldn't have asked but…"

"Normally? You're used to this sort of thing? Or do you think of me as a publicity whore?"

"No, it's just, you've never been invited onto his show and…"

"Just knock it off, Jason. I'm sorry. It's not been a good day. Just tell them I'm not interested. Thanks. Bye."

She turned back to the agent who had a devilish grin on his face.

"Something amusing?" Madison said.

"It's just nice to see someone in DC with a little heart. Most people around here lose any semblance of humanity rather quickly."

Madison breathed deeply and rocked her chair.

"No, that wasn't right. I don't treat people like that, I really don't," she said with downtrodden eyes.

"Well, under the circumstances I don't blame you."

"I appreciate your candor, Agent Robinson. If there isn't anything else I can help you with today; maybe you could contact me another time if something else pops up?"

"Yes, of course." Walter stood, buttoned his jacket, and tucked his tie into his suit.

Madison rose to accompany him to the door. Walter sensed the emotional exhaustion in her face. He held his hand out. Madison reciprocated, giving him a firm handshake.

"I realize there are rules," she began. "But if there is anything you can share in the future, please, notify me."

"I'll do what I can. Thank you for your time."

Madison held the door as Walter walked into the outer office then out to the hallway. Madison kept her hand on the door and eyed Jason who pretended not to notice as he typed away at his computer on his small, shabby desk.

"Jason, a moment please?"

"Of course, Congresswoman."

Jason stood. The rest of her staff, packed into the tiny office in various cubicles, also tried to ignore Madison.

"No need to come into my office," Madison said. "And I apologize for blowing up on you like that, it was inappropriate."

"No, it's okay, really." Jason grimaced.

"It's not. This place is filled with egomaniacs who abuse their overworked and underpaid staff more than I'd care to admit. I don't want to be that type of person. I'm just on edge today, but that's no excuse."

"Congresswoman, it's actually a perfect excuse." Tears welled in Jason's eyes. "Senator Radford was a good man. He recommended me to you. I worked with him a lot when I was with the party. He was one of the good guys."

"He was. Oh God, it doesn't seem right to refer to him in the past tense. I just had lunch with the man."

Madison's head dropped. Jason cleared his throat. "We can handle everything here for the day, why don't you head home?"

"I have a better idea, why doesn't everyone head home." Her staff perked up out of their extra small cubicles like prairie dogs.

"Thank you, Congresswoman," Jason said. "Let me just apologize again for the Goldsmith bit. I didn't want to turn it down without speaking to you first. I guess I got lost in his star power. I've tried to get you on that show before with no luck, obviously."

"It's all right; I should've told you no interviews. I suppose it was naïve of me to think the bloodsucker press would leave me alone. I'm not going to do any interviews about him, ok?"

"Sure thing," Jason replied. "But once the story is out there the news cycle will shift to the remembrance of him. Senator Radford had a lot of friends. No doubt the president will eulogize him. He's already made a statement of condolences, by the way. There might be some media outlets out there that won't hammer away on questions about what happened and just focus on his life. Any interest in that sort of thing?"

"I don't know, that's a good point. I don't think so though. Let's play it by ear."

"Okay."

"I'm headed out. Before you go would you drop some legislative drafts off in the shredder bin and make sure my schedule for next week is updated?"

Jason nodded. "You're not going to take any time off?"

"We get enough vacations around here. There will be plenty of time for that later."

Madison made it all the way to her car, unlocked the door, and sat in the driver's seat before breaking down.

She had not bawled like that since childhood.

CHAPTER 4

MADISON KICKED OFF HER SHOES THE second she walked in the door to her Alexandria, Virginia townhome. The commute was as hellish as it always is in northern Virginia—a terrible ending to an even worse day. She was accustomed to such inconveniences, having grown up in the state. Madison often remembered when she was little and things seemed much smaller with fewer people in the area. Now, it was a bustling metropolis without the actual metropolis.

Her townhome was nice but not as fine as $1.2 million should buy a person. Still though, it was a relatively quiet neighborhood, and she spent little time there, anyway. She often slept in her office or crashed at a hotel in the city for the evening. They lived there almost a year but boxes filled with belongings were still strewn about in various rooms. There were hardly any pictures on the walls and the rooms resembled staging for a real estate open house. Aside from the bedroom, kitchen, and John's office, she had little reason to venture into other areas.

After rubbing her feet and head for a few minutes, she descended to the basement in search of her husband. All the lights in the house were off except those in John's downstairs office. He had not emerged since the sun went down.

Madison spotted John Callahan reading a stock report, financial disclosure, or some other such nonsense. She sat in one of his visitor chairs. John did not notice her from behind his desk. Madison started the timer on her cellphone. She played a game where she monitored how long she could sit before John noticed her.

Tonight she passed the five minute mark before he looked up and smiled.

"Maddy, hi. I'm sorry, I didn't see you there."

He was always sorry.

"Oh, silly boy. What is so darn important now? Have you even eaten yet? It's almost 9:30."

"Oh, you know how it goes. I was waiting for you to get home before getting dinner and calling it a night. There's always so much to do."

"You never worked like this even in New York."

John leaned back with his arms behind his head in a relaxed pose. "I didn't have to. We were right in the thick of things, we were *ingrained* in everything. Now I'm playing catch up. Working from home has its advantages but I'm out of the loop by not being in a busy office."

"Offices are overrated," Madison said coldly.

"I suppose they are... sometimes. Hey, did you get any more information about the terrorist attack in Saudi Arabia? It really shook the markets today. Oil prices jumped up a tick."

"I haven't been following it much." Madison shuffled and moved her head from side to side, not really looking at anything in particular.

"Really? I thought they'd be all over it on Capitol Hill!"

"I'm sure the right people were. I had other things going on..." Madison laid her annoyance in her voice on thick.

"I couldn't believe it! 124 people dead in a police state like Saudi Arabia. And the price of oil spiked. It's so stupid. It had nothing to do with oil. The market can be so schizo-phrenic sometimes. But it will stabilize soon.

"Shuhada' Alnnabi claimed responsibility. But I thought they were Wahhabis. Isn't that what Saudi Arabia supports? Don't they give groups like that millions of dollars under the table and then publicly denounce them?"

"Yes."

"So what was that about? They're biting the hand that feeds?"

"I told you I didn't hear much about it."

"What could have been more important? Aren't we all overly worried to death of scary people like that, especially since 9/11?"

Madison sighed. John was in rare form tonight. She never tried to get on his case about anything. Their marriage was not front page of *Romance Weekly* worthy, but John was usually a perceptive guy. She kept quiet and let him drone on for a bit.

"So, if global terrorism didn't dominate your agenda was it a good day for you? Did you change the world one procedural vote at a time?" John chuckled.

Madison interlocked her fingers and sat back, relaxed her shoulders, and searched for words. She wondered if he was picking up on her irritation.

He did not.

John sat in his leather chair with a dopey smile.

"John, Boyd is dead."

John laughed. "What did he do now? Buck the party line again and vote to fund the coal industry or something? I'm sure he'll recover."

"No, John, he's *dead*. He shot himself in the head with a pistol. He's gone, deceased, not coming back."

John froze.

"How did you not hear about this?" Madison said in an elevated voice.

John stood, walked in front of his desk, and sat in the other visitor chair facing Madison. He put his hand on her knee and looked her in the eyes. His eyes glossed with moisture.

"Babe, I turned off CNBC hours ago. It was just nonstop terrorism coverage and commodities analysis. I wasn't getting anything useful so I haven't been watching the news. I'm so sorry, when did this happen?"

Madison relaxed her body and grabbed John's hand. "After I had lunch with him this afternoon."

"Dear God. Did he say anything to you?"

"Yeah."

"What?"

"He was acting odd. It's all a blur now but somehow blackmail came up."

"Blackmail? Geeze, Maddy. What the heck?"

"He said 'everyone' was being blackmailed except him."

John looked horrified. "What does that mean?"

Madison burst out of her chair, pacing back and forth. She pushed her fingers through her hair. "I don't know. But I can't stop thinking about it. Something is going on."

"Can you talk to the feds or the police about it?"

"They already stopped by. An FBI agent questioned me."

"That was fast."

"Yeah. And he specifically asked about blackmail."

John cocked his head to the side "So you told him what he said?"

"No, I left that part out."

"Why?"

"I don't know. It just didn't feel right, or relevant, or something." Whenever Madison had a mission, she made sure it was thoroughly finished. "I need to do some digging on my own I guess. It's just hard. I'm not going to be able to let this go."

"Have you called or heard from…"

"My father," Madison sneered. "No, and I don't plan on hearing from him. I certainly won't be calling him."

"Maddy, come on. They were best friends."

"They *were* best friends. They haven't spoken in some time. Their falling out came long before mine and Dad's. I never knew what happened though. They didn't speak of it. I always just thought it was over some political nonsense. It usually is around here. He didn't support some obscure judicial nominee or didn't say the right words at a press conference about God-knows-what. It's all such B.S. sometimes."

"Yet you followed in his footsteps."

Madison shot John a cold look. "Yeah, well I guess it's just in my DNA," she said sarcastically. "Plus it's all that I could relate to growing up."

Madison thought about when she first left for NYU a million years ago and how she promised herself she would never return to Virginia. She wanted something new so badly and New York seemed just far enough away and the perfect place to start over.

Of course, that was not meant to be.

Madison relaxed her shoulders. "John, do you regret moving here?"

"No, of course not. I complain a lot and I admit I miss New York sometimes. But you had an opportunity to do something great, live up to the Gladstone name while at the same time taking control of the legacy that goes with that. You're doing great things and are just getting started. I love you, Maddy. I wouldn't want to be anywhere else than right here with you."

Madison and John embraced, and held each other for what seemed like forever as they both sobbed. Then, they headed upstairs to a restless night.

CHAPTER 5

HE WAS CODE-NAMED *ADDER* AND HE had cold, gray eyes. It was somewhere between 11:00 and 11:30 p.m. as he sped quietly on a small skiff in the middle of the Gulf of Mexico. There were a few hours before the next shift started and he would need every minute.

Tonight was a new moon so it was almost pitch black. Adder planned everything down to the smallest possible detail. No one would see him coming. His radar indicated he was 300 feet from the target. He dropped the first camera buoy into the water. With a thud it hit the surface and quickly positioned itself on the target. Adder opened his display dashboard and verified the night vision was active. The weather was perfect—not a drop of rain and the waters were calm. Rarely had such a mission gone so smooth.

Adder was in the zone. The boat moved fast, and the water spritzed his face at every wave jump but his pulse remained steady. No one expected the attack, but that brought him no comfort. He relished in the fact that at any moment he could die or be killed and no one would notice or raise an alarm. To most that would be a source of extreme stress, but for Adder it was calming comfort. After his missions were over, there would be time for reflection but he pushed that aside. If you think too much about your job, especially when it is of a nefarious nature, it is best to not spend time pondering the source of your sin.

Adder circled his first target. He dropped three more buoys to form a perfect field of view. The loud sound from the target gave excellent cover. Although there were no guards or spotlights on his position, he played it like a break-in to a North Korean prison camp, which he may or may not have done. *Always expect the worst-case scenario,* he thought. That way nothing will ever take you by surprise.

Each buoy was powered and ready. The cameras were active and recording. They uploaded to a secure cloud server via satellite. He used a program secretly inserted by the CIA on a DirecTV satellite eons ago. Perhaps the legalities could be a source of debate, but launching a satellite is expensive.

During his practice runs, Adder's best time was twelve minutes. He dropped all four buoys in eleven minutes and fourteen seconds. He always rose to the occasion under pressure. Perfect.

Adder cut the motor to its lowest levels as he stealthily approached the first target. He sailed to one of the four huge pillars of the structure. He tied his boat to a nearby cable then stopped cold.

"All I'm saying is this job isn't worth the hassle," he heard someone say in the darkness near the platform.

"Whatever, you got a light?" another person replied.

Adder pulled his night vision goggles over his face. He scanned the area directly above. Two men stood on a platform fifty meters above his head. He did not see them on the approach. How clumsy, he thought. He could smell cigarette smoke for an instant before it vanished in the salty air.

"After my six months, I'm out," one man said.

"Hey, it's good money," the other man responded.

Adder remained still as the dead. He could see little of the talking men, aside from their feet on the grated platform. They were on an outside access area that probably connected to living quarters.

"It's not *that* good! There are no dang women on this tour, and if there were, they'd be so butch you'd lose your lunch."

They laughed.

"I was in boot camp, remember? After six weeks of stress and no women, you'll take the first piece of tail you see, trust me. And she won't be pretty, but you won't notice until the next morning when you're gnawing your arm off!"

They both bellowed with laughter. Adder remained still. He watched the amber color of a cigarette float delicately into the ocean and extinguish in the waves. He gazed up to see the crude men retreating through an adjacent doorway. He waited another sixty seconds before moving.

Adder checked his scuba equipment one more time. Everything looked good to go. He put on his goggles and grabbed the packages then dropped backward into the cold waters. His wetsuit kept him relatively warm, but his nerves kept him warmer. He dove below to get to work.

In his training for this mission he realized the dive would be difficult and dangerous. It was hard to practice for such conditions. At any given time he could disorient or hyperventilate and panic. He might rip off his mask in a fit of rage and lunacy or swim deeper, thinking it was toward the surface. No one ever did this type of dive without a partner to watch your back. Of course, Adder did not have that luxury. And in this case a partner would do more harm than good. Plus, he would have had to kill him afterwards, anyway. And if something did go wrong and his partner saved him, then his murder would be that much more awkward.

But this time things went smoothly. If you really do not care one way or another if you live or die then fear of death is no issue. Adder finished in forty-three minutes. It was not a great time but it was better than being discovered. The bottom of his skiff was covered in a dull fluorescent light so he could better find his way. He popped up to surface next to the boat. He removed his mask and breathed deep. The air seemed crisper.

He climbed aboard and examined the area. He checked his radar to see if anyone was around. It was a ghost town. That was as he expected.

Adder's next target was 2.3 miles away. His skiff brought him there in no time. The platform and base was slightly different. It had a Chinese flag waving somewhere in the dark air so the design would undoubtedly be different. He got to work dropping buoys.

After he finished in an even better time, he performed the same duty on two more targets. By the time he was done, the night sky was disappearing. He removed his mask and threw it to the bottom of the skiff. He then used his GPS to locate his sailboat deep in Cuban waters. In a few hours he was back and ready for business.

His boat was modest. He had stolen it from a lonely fisherman in Venezuela. But the ship was large enough to hide all his equipment and low-profile enough to keep any local patrols off his back. Adder's long black hair and mustache made him appear close enough to a Cuban. And his command of Spanish was spot-on.

He boarded the boat while dumping the equipment he would never need again. Adder headed to the bridge, turned on the engines and set a course for Cuba.

When he spotted the coastline, he cut the engines. He descended below deck to a small cabin with a laptop and a parallel monitor on a modest desk. Adder powered up and immediately saw all four targets on a digital map. The monitor showed every video feed from the buoys. They were in perfect position and recording.

Adder entered a few prompts on his laptop then stopped. He caressed the *enter* button and pushed his hand through his hair. This was it. After he pressed the button there was no turning back.

He nervously tapped the edge of his keyboard.

Adder yelled, "Just do it, you pussy." Then he took his hand off the key. He opened one of the desk drawers to pull out a bottle of Wasmund's Single Malt Whisky. He took a deep slug. Then another.

He pushed the button.

There was a slight delay before all four oil derricks were rocked with explosions from underneath the water. As they slowly sank, he could see men scattering onto lifeboats. Oil seeped to the surface, turning the waters Adder had just dived, pure black. Then the water caught fire in various places as the now crippled platforms burned and sank. Although he was miles away, it did not take long before the scent of the burning oil assaulted his nostrils.

He waited until each oil derrick had completely submerged before stopping the videos. Adder entered another prompt and each buoy went dark. They were programmed to explode and sink.

Adder opened his email and looked over the message written in Arabic he had already re-read a dozen times. Then he put each video into a zip file and attached it to the email.

Adder took another slug from the Wasmund's bottle. He paced back and forth, drawing deep from the bottle.

He rubbed his face and rocked back and forth as his hands shook uncontrollably.

And then something happened that had only occurred one other time on a mission—he cried. He bawled uncontrollably and curled into a little ball. But the tremendous loss of life and total destruction committed by his hand was not top of mind.

He breathed quickly while repeating, "No choice, no choice," over and over again like a madman.

It took fifteen minutes before he could get to his feet. Adder then calmed, approached the laptop and hit *send*. His mission was complete.

The next time the hackers at *Wikileaks* opened their email they would get the scoop of a lifetime. And everything would change forever.

It was done.

"What have I done?" Adder said under his breath.

CHAPTER 6

TURN ON NEWS, RIGHT NOW.

The urgency from Jason's text message was not lost on Madison as she was busy dressing and preparing to leave for the office. She scurried downstairs to find her husband John already in his office. He stood, watching the television.

"Hey, Maddy, did you hear?"

"Hear what?" She replied.

"There was a major terrorist attack in the Gulf of Mexico. Four oil derricks exploded at the same time."

"Oh, dear lord. How many people were killed?"

"Not sure yet, but it isn't good. Not only that but oil is gushing from the bottom of the ocean in every location. The entire Gulf will be contaminated."

Madison sighed. "Turn it up, please?" she asked John, who clicked "the volume up" a few notches.

The anchor was visibly upset as she continued, "... and the more we learn the more gruesome the details have become. *WikiLeaks* released video of each explosion with a statement indicating it was sent from a terrorist organization last night. The video is vivid and disturbing. What you're about to see is a clip of an oil derrick as a loud boom is heard in the background. Then, the derrick shakes. You see it wobble and descend into the ocean as fire erupts and engulfs the entire platform. In a matter of minutes it sinks into a ball of fire. Workers jump into the waters to avoid the flames. If you're faint of heart, please look away."

The anchor's description did not do the carnage justice. Oil bubbled to the surface and caught fire. Mini explosions all over the derricks brought the massive structures down like they were made of paper. People burned alive as they leaped to their deaths.

"And now we have just received word that President Wilson will make a brief statement from the White House," the anchor chimed in. The camera then swiped over to the presidential podium in the Rose Garden at the White House. President Lloyd Wilson entered from the back doors and walked to his perch alongside the sound of snapping cameras.

President Wilson wore a somber expression. His face showed a cold seriousness. He wore a navy blue suit with a power red tie. Wilson nailed the look required of the leader of the free world. His perfectly quaffed hair and commanding persona emphasized his greatest traits and distracted from his relative youth for the position.

He placed his hands on the podium and looked left, then right. He cleared his throat and began.

"This morning, America woke to the news of another horrendous act of terror," he said. "This act was perpetrated by cowards who believe fear can intimidate the United States of America. I am here to say there is nothing further from the truth. I hope that every one of you will join me in praying for the victims, their families, and that these criminals will soon be brought to justice.

"After my daily national security briefing, I directed the FBI, CIA, and our entire intelligence community to work night and day until those responsible are arrested. They assured me that this will be the definition of quick justice. We will find those responsible, I assure you of that.

"At approximately five this morning, four oil derricks suffered a total collapse after explosive charges were triggered underwater at fault points causing them to sink within minutes. This deliberate act required knowledge and precision and was no random act of violence. It was committed with the express intent of terrorizing the population. We have not yet determined how many people lost their lives but the final number will be nothing short of catastrophic.

"An American company owned two of these derricks. The others were operated by Chinese and Russian state-owned companies. I have spoken with the president of Russia and the premier of China. I offered to share whatever intelligence we learn from the incident and asked them to reciprocate.

"We have a serious oil leakage problem in the Gulf of Mexico. At this point, we are optimistic we can limit exposure on beaches and the ocean. We have discussed the use of skimmer ships and controlled burns to keep the oil from inflicting even more damage. The CEOs of each oil company are also working on plans to stem the flow of oil. Unfortunately, they have never fathomed such a situation. There are no contingency plans in place nor were there adequate safety measures enabled to stop the oil. Before today, no one believed a terrorist attack of this magnitude and design could occur. This marks the beginning of a new reality.

"I cannot stress enough that the situation is dire. Millions of barrels of oil are seeping into the ocean at an astronomical level. If we cannot plug these holes, the devastation will become cataclysmic."

John rubbed his face. "Oh, God, this is bad. The markets will take a complete dump this morning. It will be a long one for me." Already stock figures and company outlooks swirled through his head. Every world event made an impact on some sector of the stock market. Skittish investors in sectors unrelated to the oil industry would take a hit. For a broker, it was easily the most frustrating part of the job. You can make all the correct calls and forecasts but when something like this occurs everything gets thrown out the window.

Madison ignored him as she focused on the president. "What is he thinking with all this doom and gloom? People are scared; they need comfort and confidence, not warnings of destruction." Every political instinct she possessed stemmed from years of dealing with crises that affected not only public policy but her family in deep and personal ways. The political game players were ruthless and it took a keen personality to navigate the waters.

The president continued, "We also know now, as *WikiLeaks* foolishly released, that terrorists involved in the bombings recorded evidence of their crimes. I hope you will not watch these videos or pass them around on social media. To do so will only embolden their hate-filled agenda."

Madison grumbled, "Well, too late for that!" She recalled sitting next to Wilson during her fundraiser smiling like a teenybopper. On the inside though, she could not believe how someone with so little personal appeal made it to the White House. His supporters lapped up every word like it was Gospel. Wilson could contradict himself within the same sentence and yet his followers would willingly support both propositions. It drove the right batty. They would call him on his inconsistencies but never seem to get any traction from an adoring media. Madison was well aware that criticisms of the president would go undiscussed on the Sunday Morning Talk Shows.

"I also wanted to comment," the president continued, "on the fact that a known terror group, Shuhada' Alnnabi, has claimed responsibility. This is a name I am sure you are well aware of as they have committed atrocities over the world for years since their publicized split with *Al Qaeda*. We are still trying to confirm their part in the attack. But if true, then my message to them is that their acts of violence will not go without an answer, and they will never win.

"To freedom-loving Americans, I urge you to remember that not all Muslims are terrorists. We must never forget that Islam is a peaceful religion. Most Muslims are just like you and me. They work, vote, practice their religion, and go to school. They want nothing more than to live their lives.

"And let me be clear, this administration will not tolerate bigotry or acts of revenge against our Muslim brothers and sisters. This is not the time for short-sighted and shameful acts of hatred against people who have nothing to do with the Gulf attacks. I urge all Americans to stand hand in hand with the Middle East and the Muslim community. Any crimes committed against Muslims will be treated as a hate crime and perpetrators will be prosecuted to the fullest extent of the law."

President Wilson showed the most fire of his speech during these lines.

"I cannot express how important it is that we come together and not seek to blame others for which they are not responsible. After the 9/11/01 attacks, it horrified me to see acts of cowardice against fellow Americans because of their religious beliefs. I will not see such days return. Today is a day for unity, not hatred.

"I will keep you apprised of the situation in the Gulf of Mexico. Do not fear. My fellow Americans, thank you and God bless."

Madison flipped off the TV and threw the remote onto the sofa with a loud thud. John gave her an odd look. She hesitated then met his eyes and said, "What a pussy."

John laughed.

Madison joined in too and shook her head.

"He did a rather nice fundraiser for you," John reminded her. He could not stop chuckling. Madison was known for her straight talk. John loved her for it and was surprised it had not put her in more danger politically. "What didn't you like?"

"Yeah, well, he's not here and you're not CNN so what do I care? For one, he offered no plan," she started, "and second, he spent most of his time lecturing scared Americans about being nice to Muslims?"

John raised an eyebrow. "You don't think they should?"

"Stop it. Of course I do," Madison swatted at John. "But everyone knows not all Muslims are terrorists for God's sake. We need not a reminder of that. It's the constitutional professor mindset in the president he can't shake. We don't need a lecturer, we need a leader. Show us he's doing something about the problem, not telling us to be nice to each other. It makes me sick. What a buffoon."

"I don't suppose you'll repeat that in public, eh?"

"I don't suppose I will."

CHAPTER 7

"THANKS FOR PICKING ME UP, JASON," Madison said to her chief of staff who stood next to his Toyota Prius as she exited her house. "I just could not face this morning's traffic after the time I've had lately."

"Of course, boss. Glad to help."

"You still have this thing?" She said as she slid into the passenger seat. Jason smiled and closed the door after she settled. He walked to the driver's side, opened the door and entered. Jason put his hands on the steering wheel and casually turned to her with a sly look.

"Whatever do you mean?" He smirked.

"Why do you drive this oversized *Power Wheels* car?"

He put the car in gear and drove. "I can't believe you're ridiculing my baby here. This is a high-performance vehicle."

Madison laughed. "Stop it."

"Hey, it's great on gas mileage and the optics are great for you. Your base loves to see you caring about the environment, doing your part, blah, blah, blah, etcetera, etcetera."

"If only my base knew most electricity comes from coal plants they might not be too enthused on the environmental implication."

"Yes, well, perception is the reality in politics. It's part of the phony side."

Madison nodded. The *phony side* was an ongoing debate she had with Jason regarding the state of politics in

America. They both agreed there were two sides to government with the other being the *substance*, as they called it.
The substance was not sexy. It was the days of haggling over
lines in bills that would get no press coverage but had the
most impact on American life. It was deals made with the
opposition that no one ever discussed but kept the government running. It was the phone call you made to a widow
of a slain military veteran who lived in your district. The
phony side was what everyone despised yet also craved. It
was dumbing down complex political issues to slogans and
one-word rallying cries like "deregulation" or founding a
political movement on something that sounds like a pizza
commercial catchphrase.

Madison detested the phony side. But it was a necessary evil, and she knew it. As much as it irked her, it was
only about 10 percent of the job. To a casual observer
that might seem small but most of her work was out of
the public eye. In fact, if the public knew about the other
90 percent then they might be outraged. But of course,
nothing would get done.

Madison pondered this as she sat in silence as Jason's
Prius made its way through the most horrendous daily
traffic on the planet. The sun was still rising but the *mixing
bowl* was already a disaster. She actually preferred the traffic
in New York to the DC area. Nothing compared to this
vehicular monstrosity.

"So what's on tap today?" Madison asked.

"You've got a meeting with Peter Baylor."

"Really? Did I approve that?" Madison shuffled
through emails and other messages on her phone.

"Were you supposed to?"

"I suppose not, just wish I had the option to say no."

Jason laughed. "What's wrong with Peter?"

"Oh come on. He's an ass." Madison looked away from her phone toward a smirking Jason. She glanced in the back to see random changes of clothes, a few files strewn about, and some random candy bar wrappers. It was a typical backseat for a DC operative.

"Yeah, I guess he is. He's probably looking for another job now and wants your help. But if that's the case, he's moving quick."

"He doesn't need my help. Chiefs of staff are recycled on Capitol Hill more than bottles... no offense."

"Hey, if it's true I can't get mad."

"So what does he want, anyway?"

"No idea," Jason said. "He refused to tell me. He might angle for my job I guess. I put it on the schedule since he worked for Senator Radford for so long. But if he's such an *ass* as you say, why did he work with him so long?"

Madison bobbed her head. "Simple, he's effective. You don't win points in this city for style. You have to get things done."

"No question about that." Jason finally slid the car into the HOV lane. He was rewarded with an increase of about five miles per hour.

"So, why isn't the committee on Energy and Commerce meeting this morning?" Madison asked. She rolled her eyes after noticing a woman in an adjacent car putting on makeup while driving.

"After the terrorist attack, the president threw everyone for a curve with such an early morning message. No one was expecting him to act so quickly."

"'Act' isn't the word I would use." In the next car they passed a man who was reading a book while driving. He held the book at the top of the steering wheel and drove with his other hand. Madison thought little of that encounter. She had seen it many times before.

"Well, *speak* on the matter anyway. I guess everyone assumed he would talk about it tonight in prime time. He must've wanted to get his message in the news cycle right away. But regardless, the committee meeting is scheduled for 3:00 today. Hopefully the dust has cleared and everyone isn't running around in circles with no answers."

When Madison and Jason made it to the office, Peter Baylor was already sitting in the visitor's chair across from Madison's desk. The presumption annoyed her, but she remained calm. Madison took her time getting to her desk. Peter was tapping his fingers on the arm of the chair. At first, she assumed he was nervous but then she remembered he was always in a state of over-caffeination.

"Hello, Peter," she said, forgoing the customary hand-shake as she took a seat at her desk and shuffled papers. She quickly noticed the morning news clips set out by her press secretary. She shoved them aside and gave Peter her attention.

"Congresswoman," he said in a gruff voice.

Peter was a few years older than Madison. He had spent fifteen years on Capitol Hill, which is worth two or three lifetimes in politics. Peter was overweight but not morbidly obese. His salt and pepper hair was retreating from his scalp. He always ate bad food and he sweated—a lot.

"I know you must be as devastated about Boyd's death as I am," she said. "It has been exceedingly difficult for me, for all of us. I'm still reeling."

"I know what you mean," Peter replied. "And no matter. It is what it is."

Madison wanted to punch him in his smug face. "Now, what can I do for you?" Madison crossed her legs and sat back, trying to prevent her eyes from drawing toward the daily press clips.

"Let me be blunt. The governor is dragging his feet in calling for a special election. He will not appoint anyone before the next general election." Peter leaned forward. His girth made him appear rather uncomfortable in Madison's small chairs.

"You're kidding," Madison said, surprised. "This is a golden chance for Republicans to take the seat back even if it's temporary."

"I'm well aware of that," Peter said with annoyance. "But he's stuck. His people have convinced him there is no one strong enough to hold on to the seat even as a short-lived incumbent. Plus the Democratic party is already playing the guilt card, insinuating that he would take advantage of a terrible situation."

"And that's working?" Madison guffawed.

"Surprisingly. His people have convinced him that the GOP would appear as above the fray, so to speak, in running for an election fair and square."

"That's beyond stupid. We'd appoint someone in a heartbeat."

"Well, that's politics."

"Yes it is."

Peter straightened his posture and adjusted his tie. "And that's why I wanted to talk to you today." He actually appeared to stop sweating. Madison wondered if he had so much experience sweating he knew how to control it in the face of pressure. That would certainly be quite a talent.

"Look, let me stop you right there," she started. "I'm not going to run for Boyd's seat. I just got here and I have things I want to accomplish. I don't want to run for higher office. And the timing of all this is too much. Let's bury the man first before jockeying for his job."

"Well…" Peter smiled nervously and cracked his neck.

Madison raised an eyebrow and cleared her throat. "What is it?"

"I want to run."

In an instant, Madison saw right through this large, sweaty man. She searched for words but all that came was, "Hmm."

"The party approached me. They want to pull on heartstrings just like after Gabby Giffords was shot and Ron Barber took her seat."

"He didn't last long," Madison remarked.

"No, but I'm better than Ron Barber," Peter said with a very DC smugness. The longer you stayed on Capitol Hill the larger your ego.

Madison suddenly remembered why she did not care for Peter Baylor. Ignoring that last comment, Madison said, "So what do you want from me?"

"I want your support. Senator Radford was your close friend. Everyone knows that. Your endorsement would go a long way in Virginia. I need your political organization to help get things moving. The rumor is the election will be on the ballot in November with the local state races. That only gives us a few months to get ready. I need you on my team. I'd like you to introduce me at my announcement speech and then go from there. Within two days of the governor declaring the election, I need you on that podium with me. My campaign manager will give you all the details in the next day or so. Do you want her to coordinate with you or with Jason?"

"Now wait a minute," she said as she stood. "You're assuming I'll endorse you." Madison put her hands on her hips the way her mother always did whenever she had done something bad as a child.

Peter gave her a look of befuddlement. "Why wouldn't you?"

"Look, I haven't thought for thirty seconds about who will run for Boyd's seat. I'm not ready to commit just yet. To be honest, I'd prefer to sit this one out. The man just died for God's sake. This is morbid."

Peter's face turned beet red as he said, "Come on, Madison!"

She took note he called her by her name instead of "Congresswoman."

"You can't sit this one out. It's an election. You're a politician. Politicians don't sit out elections!" The sweat from his head caused his crusty-gelled hair to lose some of its staying power.

"I haven't committed to anything. I need time. Look, Peter, I've got a lot on my plate right now. And to be honest the talk of politics still seems inappropriate after Boyd's death." She wanted to wag her finger right in his face. But that was also her mother's move. And Madison would be damned if she turned into her mother, as much as she loved her though.

"Maybe to you!" He stood and smoothed the arms of his suit coat. "This is the big leagues. We move on because that's what the public demands. This election will influence the political structure of this country for decades. You can't sit on the fence. I'll expect you to come around soon."

He was real close to a fingerwagging.

"You know what, Peter... you can get the hell out of my office." She pointed at her door with gritted teeth.

His face froze in a portrait of sheer contempt. "I'll let that go because I wouldn't have lasted long in this business if I didn't have thick skin. I'll be in touch."

Madison rolled her eyes after he turned toward the door. He stormed out as Jason was giving instructions to the intern manning the front desk.

"Everything all right, Peter?" he asked.

"I look forward to working with you soon," he replied making his way to the hall.

Jason popped his head into Madison's office. "So am I being replaced or demoted?" he queried with that same Jason smirk.

Madison was perusing the daily press clips. She locked eyes with Jason and replied, "No, he's running for Boyd's seat and wants my support. I told him I'd think about it. If anyone asks, you know nothing."

"Got it."

"What's next?"

"Well," Jason said, "the Shuhada' Alnnabi video is now being broadcast on the cable news channels. They keep showing it in a loop every hour."

Madison sighed. "All right, I guess we have to watch their propaganda for when we're asked about it."

Jason flipped on the television in her office. Reginald Goldsmith appeared on the screen wearing a deep-V-neck t-shirt as he stood on a beach somewhere in the Gulf of Mexico. Reginald loved the *man-of-action* look. He was dashing though for an older man with white hair.

"We can now independently confirm that Shuhada' Alnnabi is responsible for the oil derrick attacks," he said in his trademark booming voice. "Earlier this morning, they released the following video. We will now show it in its entirety. While we don't want to promote this hateful terrorist organization, we feel that the public has a right to know. Therefore our team made the courageous decision to air the tape. Viewer discretion is advised."

The camera shot on Reginald faded as a man wearing a balaclava in an extreme close-up came onto screen in a grainy video feed. He said:

"We are Shuhada' Alnnabi and we are many. The infidels of the Great Satan America along with the criminals in Russia and China are feeling the wrath of the great sword of Islam today. We have struck a defiant blow into the power centers of greed in which you fuel the machines of war against the great people of Islam. This is the only warning we shall give before you come face-to-face with our destructive force.

"We struck the mall in Saudi Arabia and now we sunk the oil platforms in the oceans. This is the beginning of the bloodshed in the name of Allah. We demand that the western powers remove their machines of war from the Middle East and declare their lands in the name of Allah. Oil is a black curse on our lands that has made whores out of weak Muslims. We seek to remove this poison from our lands by destroying the industries that prey on their weakness. The king of Saudi Arabia must abdicate and pledge allegiance to Shuhada' Alnnabi. Wahhabism has become corrupt with the interests of greedy government mercenaries. It is time for the Caliphate to take his place as the one true leader of the world. You have been warned.

"Allahu Akbar."

CHAPTER 8

MADISON HURRIED DOWN THE CORRIDOR OF the Rayburn building on Capitol Hill. She normally walked with an aide in tow but this time she traversed alone with nothing but disturbed thoughts. The chairman of the Committee on Energy and Commerce had called an emergency meeting to discuss the ongoing oil spill crisis in the Gulf of Mexico. Madison always was as close to on-time or early for such gatherings.

The intrepid congresswoman was eager to attend what would hopefully be a productive debate on how to plug the hole in the ocean floor spewing millions of gallons of oil. She felt energized and ready for updates on a problem that the government might actually be able to fix. But her motivation took a hit when she reached the door to the committee briefing. There, Agent Walter Robinson stood with his leg fixed on the adjacent wall like a sideways V.

"Good morning, Mr. Robinson," Madison said as she reached for the door handle to the conference room.

"Congresswoman, could I have just a moment of your time?" he replied. Madison removed her hand from the doorknob and stepped back.

"Listen, this meeting is important, can this wait?"

"I wish it could. I realize I have no legal authority to stop you. If you're on your way to do congressional business, then you can break whatever law you want, least of all ignoring an FBI agent."

45

"Don't be such a drama queen," Madison retorted. "What do you want?"

Agent Robinson scoffed. "Yes, of course. I just had a couple of questions if you don't mind." He removed his notebook from his jacket pocket and flipped through some pages.

"Go on." Madison wanted to scream. She hated being caught off guard. On the campaign trail, an operative from her opponent ambushed her with a camera as she left the auditorium of their final debate. The media claimed she was tense as the cameraman peppered her with inane questions. Madison felt she should have been commended for not knocking his block off. Politics.

"I understand that you're busy with the terrorist attack and the oil spill. If I was a more important agent, I would be assigned to such things myself. As it were, I must spend my days harassing you." Walter opened his mouth slightly as if waiting for a reaction.

Madison took a breath and straightened her back. "Get to the point."

Agent Robinson cleared his throat. "I wanted to get a better sense of your relationship with Senator Boyd Radford. He was a complicated man who had many allies and enemies. I will keep everything you say confidential as long as no real crime has been committed. So I need to know how close were you, really?"

"I hope you're not insinuating we had an inappropriate relationship."

"I'm not insinuating anything."

Madison crossed her arms. She wondered if a representative could face charges for smacking an FBI agent as long as she was on her way to official business. "Boyd was like a father, okay? He was close with my real dad for years.

After a while they had a falling out and stopped speaking. But Boyd was always there for me. He helped me in my political aims and legislative goals. I miss him. He was more than just a colleague. I would have done just about anything for him. And it kills me he's gone."

"I understand." Walter scribbled something in his notebook.

"No you don't," Madison snapped back. "If you did, then you wouldn't be asking me such ridiculous questions."

Walter put his notebook back in his coat pocket. "I understand this is difficult. I don't want to upset you but I need to ask a few, well, uncomfortable questions."

"Come on already. I'm an elected official who has done nothing wrong. I want to know why Boyd killed himself more than anyone but this is getting ridiculous. What are you trying to prove?"

"I get it, I do. The problem is that the senator had some unusual circumstances surrounding his death. I'm not at liberty to discuss that in-depth but I need to collect as much information as possible." Passersby in the hallway glanced at the pair as their voices elevated. Some pretended to fool around on their phones.

Madison tapped her feet and calmed as she noticed the gawkers. She checked the clock on her cellphone. It was almost time for the committee hearing.

"Get on with it," she said in a much softer tone.

"Did your relationship ever cross any, well, boundaries?"

"No." Madison made a fist and squeezed.

"Do you want me to," Walter paused as Madison gave him a menacing look, "...elaborate at all?"

"No. I get it. We never had an affair. To insinuate that is such a grotesque item for you to attack me with."

Walter held up both his hands in a surrender pose. "Hey, I'm doing my job."

Madison squinted. She could feel the eyes of every person passing by. This probably was not the most inappropriate conversation ever heard on Capitol Hill, but it was definitely the worst one Madison had been a part. "I don't know where this is coming from and I don't care," she said pointing a finger in the middle of his chest. "Let me tell you something about Boyd Radford. I have always had a complicated relationship with the political legend that is my arrogant father. He was one of the most popular governors Virginia ever had, and probably could have been president if he had not gone off the rails in later years. I worked on his staff when I was younger but when I branched out on my own, he never let it go.

"When I ran for office, he refused to endorse me. I didn't even care, but the media did. The stories became national headlines and almost cost me my election. Just before November, he sent out some lackey to explain that he had health problems but could not elaborate further. He abandoned me the way he thought I abandoned him.

"Boyd Radford saved my campaign. He not only endorsed me but he gave me access to his fundraising and grassroots database. If it weren't for him I would have been toast. He did it because he believed in me and thought I could make a difference. And unlike every other drone on Capitol Hill, he never asked for anything in return. Boyd had more guts than anyone I ever knew and not only am I heartbroken but I know the country is worse off with him gone."

Agent Robinson stared at the floor and shuffled his feet.

"Now if you excuse me, I have to go. If you have any other questions submit them in writing to my chief of staff."

Robinson moved out of the way and ushered her into the room with an outstretched hand.

Madison was not one of the first people at the hearing as she had hoped. Instead, she looked to be one of the last. The chairman, a pudgy congressman from Florida named Gonzalez, was already briefing the committee.

"...So it seems we have a real problem on our hands. Forgetting the national security implications for a minute, the immediate threat is stopping the gushing oil from polluting the Gulf of Mexico and our shorelines. The fact of the matter is that we don't have any contingency plans for the collapse of an oil derrick, let alone four. Around 4,000 barrels of oil, amounting to 168,000 gallons, are leaking into the ocean each day. The oil sheen on the surface stretches for close to 1,000 miles.

"While we work on plugging the holes, we have deployed the On-Scene Coordinator with the Environmental Protection Agency, who is evaluating options from a Coast Guard vessel near the American derrick that went down. They have already declared the federal government must get involved with the cleanup and have activated the Regional Response Team and the Environmental Response Team. The National Oceanic and Atmospheric Administration Support Coordinators are also at the scene. But the EPA is running the show for now."

Madison quietly took a seat. Half the room was listening to the briefing. The other half was on their phones or giving orders to nearby aides. Most of them probably had their minds on how they can spin this to their advantage in the next election.

"They have already determined," Gonzalez moaned on, "that skimming and dispersants will have a minimal effect but they are still being attempted. The next option is a controlled burn of the oil on the surface. Burning has been an effective method in the past to remove large amounts of oil after a spill. Despite our efforts, the OSC expects oil to wash up on the shores of Louisiana within two to four days. The governor has already issued a state of emergency and FEMA is mobilizing.

"I am told the president will issue an executive order later today halting new offshore drilling until the EPA and Congress can review and approve safeguards. Right now estimates for the overall cost of the cleanup are in the billions.

"The owners of each derrick have formed a working committee to share ideas and resources. They are positioning to dig relief wells next to the gushing holes but that will take days to complete and there is no guarantee of success. A containment dome is on its way from a manufacturer in New York. If that is successful, other domes will be made available. In the meantime, the companies are trying to clog the holes with mud, debris, and other objects. So far nothing has been successful but they are working fast."

The committee members burst with gasps. Some even cried. Others were red with anger. Gonzalez raised his hands and begged the members to calm.

"Listen, this is still early and my office will get you reports whenever we get an update from the OSC. In the meantime, we are reaching out to the CEOs of each company to schedule them to testify on why they had no plans for this eventuality. Needless to say, some of these companies will be suffering for a long time. There may even be indictments."

Madison almost jumped out of her seat. "Excuse me, Chairman," she almost yelled, "Why are we focusing on these companies and not the terrorists who committed this crime?"

"That's not our role in this, Congresswoman," Gonzalez said sharply.

"Cut the crap. Everyone's number-one concern should be finding those responsible while making sure they don't hit us again. What is being done about increasing security for other oil derricks?" The room paused in amazement. Gonzalez hesitated and scanned the room to see all eyes were on this tenacious freshman congresswoman from Virginia.

"Again, Congresswoman, that's not our role here. I'm sure the FBI and CIA are working overtime to find those responsible. The Coast Guard is probably adding additional security measures as well—"

"Wait, I'm sorry, *probably*? You don't know?" Madison widened her eyes and leaned forward with a look that screamed *are you serious?*

Gonzalez crossed his arms. "Look, Madison, this is a difficult situation for everyone. We're all under a lot of pressure. But as you will come to find out, when you've been here longer than a few months, problems arise all the time. Half of what we do is put out fires, so to speak. Losing your cool will not accomplish anything. And you should learn sooner rather than later that most politicians wait until cameras are *on* before grandstanding."

Madison pounded her fist on the table. "Grandstanding? Now listen here, you little—"

Before she could finish Congresswoman Fran Norris, the ranking Republican on the committee and ten-term veteran, interjected. "Why don't we adjourn and wait for updates from the OSC. Thank you, chairman, for the update."

Madison shook her head and headed for the door. Other committee members milled around in various conversations. She could feel the penetrating gaze from Gonzalez as she headed toward the door. Before reaching the exit, she felt a hand on her arm. She turned her head to see a smiling Fran Norris.

"You are quite the firebrand," she said.

Madison tried to respond but all she could muster was a sigh.

"You're right. About what you said, I mean. I thought you should know," Norris said with another smile. "Most people on the Hill don't get that kind of brashness until at least their third term." Fran had a grandmotherly image and tone. Her constituency thought of her as a wise sage who had been around long enough to see and hear a thing or twelve. She was a shark on the campaign trail and knew everyone in DC. Fran was also stylish for an older woman. She almost always wore a colorful scarf—her trademark look. The glasses on the end of her nose completed the ensemble.

"It pissed me off," Madison replied. "The whole thing. Terrorists are running amok and we're targeting CEOs? Come on."

"Well that's the rub, isn't it?" Fran took Madison's hand in a comforting gesture. "We all feel powerless after an event like this occurs. We want to do something. And we don't have as much power as we think, at least on this committee."

"I suppose I should have just kept my mouth shut?"

"Oh goodness no! You said what a lot of us were thinking. Well, at least on my side of the aisle." Fran winked. "I am on my way to a classified briefing about Shuhada' Alnnabi. It's only for members of the Homeland

Security Committee. But I think I have enough clout these days to sneak you in. What do you say?"

Madison's anger dissipated. A broad smile revealed her eagerness. "Yes, yes, of course. It would honor me. Thank you."

"Let's go then. It's being held a few levels below."

CHAPTER 9

FRAN LED MADISON DOWN A TIGHT corridor away from the bustle on Capitol Hill. They did not speak as Fran moved without a care in the world. Madison hid her anxiousness. They approached a small staircase and descended four floors to a poorly lit platform, one level above the basement floor. Madison thought it a storage area for janitorial equipment but close to the last step was an unassuming door with light shining from the crack at the bottom.

Fran waltzed to the right of the door. She produced an ID card from her pocket and waved it in front of a keypad. A corresponding beep followed with the sound of the door unlocking. Fran pushed it open.

They entered a hallway with ten closed doors on each side. The decor was plain and appeared to not have been updated since the 1970s. The floor was a brown carpet almost as hideous as the mustard-yellow walls. The Formica doors were garnished with cheap door knobs. It looked like something you'd see in an old dentist's office. It was terribly lit and only the hum of an unseen air conditioner pervaded the air.

For a moment she thought Fran was pulling some freshman-hazing prank. She almost voiced a protest when Fran opened the third door on the left to a packed state-of-the-art room that put the hallway to shame. There were multiple television sets with muted news programs and a huge wall of interactive surface boards at the front of the room. The seating was arranged like a college lecture hall with rows of tables and chairs looking down on a main stage area.

"Here, come take a seat," Fran said as she led Madison to two empty chairs in the middle of the room.

Madison recognized several people in the room; some by acquaintance, others by reputation. But she had never seen the four people milling around on the main stage. They stood in a semi-circle exchanging documents and chatting. A frumpy-looking man mingled in the middle, nodding as the others spoke to him while he reviewed papers in a manila folder. He was a large man with an over-worked face. The man's suit had the appearance of being recently slept in and his 5 o'clock shadow was unkempt. His tie listed to one side. He rubbed his temple with his index finger.

After a few minutes, the man motioned for his aides to take their seats. Without protest, they sat. The room quieted almost on cue as the elected officials settled.

The man cleared his throat and with an emotionless face cut right to the chase. "Shuhada' Alnnabi is responsible for the attacks in the Gulf of Mexico, this we know." His voice sounded like he had spent years smoking cigarettes and washing out the taste with hard liquor. "However, this is not something our intelligence assets had on their radar. For the past few years, the CIA and the DIA have been working assets connected to Shuhada' Alnnabi in Saudi Arabia, Russia, China, and Yemen. We can also confirm that the intelligence agencies in those countries have been covertly supplying Shuhada' Alnnabi with weapons, funding, tactical information, and other aid for years in attempts to destabilize Western interests."

Madison almost fell out of her chair. Fran calmly grabbed her wrist, leaned in, and whispered, "You will hear things you would not have known for years on the Hill, if ever. Take it in stride and never let anyone here think you don't already know everything you're about to hear or they'll eat you alive."

Madison nodded and interlaced her fingers on her lap. She tried her best poker face but in her heart she felt like she stuck out like a naked woman in the men's locker room.

"...and needless to say," the frumpy man continued, "These government agencies are not pleased, especially Russia and China who were hit in the attack on the oil derricks. Saudi Arabia believes Shuhada' Alnnabi is also responsible for the recent mall attack in Riyadh and have severed funding to the group. China and Russia have already initiated plans to take out a few of their training sites, secret bank accounts, and have eyed their leaders for assassination.

"But we believe there is more to this story. Something just does not add up. We are not aware of any new funding mechanism for Shuhada' Alnnabi aside from opium in Afghanistan. That operation has not expanded nor is it sufficient to fund the growing Shuhada' Alnnabi army. It makes no sense they would bite the hand that feeds their murderous ambitions.

"Electrical communication goes dark before an attack like clockwork. It is standard for every terrorist cell to get off the airwaves, Internet, and cease all forms of communication before a major operation like the Gulf of Mexico attack takes place. Every attack since 9/11 has followed this pattern. Our SigInt capabilities are such that we are sure we have at least seventy-five to eighty-five percent of Shuhada' Alnnabi communications documented and accounted for in every hemisphere. Before this attack though, the regular chatter did not cease. It did not increase. It maintained the same level it normally does. We have repeatedly combed through the raw files and there has been no mention of an attack in Riyadh or the Gulf.

"So, here comes the scary part, ladies and gentlemen. We believe Shuhada' Alnnabi is going through some internal struggles for power or, and the more likely scenario, is that a splinter cell has broken off and taken their acts of terrorism to a new level. This may be at the behest of a senior leader working alone or an entirely different cell that just got too big for their britches. Either way, it would force Shuhada' Alnnabi to claim responsibility or risk looking weak if they knew for sure one of their operatives perpetrated these attacks."

All over the room sidebars erupted. The man giving the briefing looked up and down with a face filled with disgust before raising his hands and saying, "Okay, Okay, listen. This splinter cell idea is just a theory. But we're working our assets across the globe to get more information."

Madison tapped her fingers on the table with one hand and cupped the side of her face with the other. Her leg bounced up and down.

"Right now," he said, "we will continue to look into this splinter cell possibility and come up with an organizational chart. Then we'll brief you when the president decides on how to strike back. If he decides to strike back." The man could not hide his distaste as he said "if."

His aides surrounded him again as the room stood into chattering panoply. Fran moved her chair back when Madison shot up and said, "Excuse me."

The room silenced. She could feel the stares from every direction. At that moment, she realized no one questioned anything the man said, or even addressed him by name. This was a deep-state actor who was not to be trifled with.

The man raised an eyebrow as he gazed at Madison but said nothing. The jaw of one of his aides actually dropped.

Madison scanned the room, stood up taller, and asked, "This is obviously the second target in a short period. Do you have any idea what they might target next? That seems to be the most important thing to figure out, don't you think?"

The man at the front of the room showed no emotion on his face. He crossed his arms and replied smugly, "How did you get in here?"

"I'm Representative Madison Glad—"

"Representative Gladstone from Virginia," the man interrupted. "I asked how you got in here. You don't have the proper clearances."

Before Madison could answer Fran interjected, "She's a guest of mine. And we would all appreciate it if you stopped dicking around and answer her question because it's a damn good one."

"Hm," the man sighed to himself. He looked down his nose with a hardened gaze then said, "Look, terrorism is a difficult animal to predict. We're dealing with fanatics with sociopathic tendencies. They make the mob look like pussycats. It's not so simple—"

This time it was Madison's turn to interrupt. "So," she began, "you don't have a clue, do you?"

The man tensed. He nervously adjusted his tie back and forth before replying, "We're working on that."

"Yes, that would be a good idea."

Madison stomped out of the hushed room. She headed toward the door to the stairwell when she realized she was alone. She had instinctively expected Fran to follow her. Why though, she could not say. Madison froze as she watched the door for what seemed like a rather long time.

Finally, Fran exited with a smile on her face waving to some colleagues. She turned to see Madison waiting.

"Oh, there you are," Fran said. "I thought you'd be long gone by now."

Madison approached with hands out and palms up. "Listen, I wasn't trying to cause trouble. It seems like today there are a lot of people missing the point."

"Welcome to Washington," Fran said with a devilish smile.

"Yeah, I'm learning quickly."

Fran chuckled. "I'm proud of you. That's how you get things done in a town that gets nothing done. And when it comes to national security there isn't any room for B.S. but the people around here always find a way to muck it up."

"How are you not frustrated by that?" Madison said. They walked side by side back up the way they entered.

"You get used to it and then adapt," Fran answered in her grandmotherly tone. "We're all playing the game here. You know, the way you showed prowess in there when it comes to terrorism makes me think you'd make a tremendous Republican."

Madison laughed. "That would be the day. My father would have an aneurism."

Fran grinned as if Madison and she had shared a wicked inside joke. They made their way up the stairs into the main hallway. "Behind closed doors," she whispered, "and away from the cameras and campaign rhetoric, party is all relative around here. You can denounce someone on the Hill and then play golf with them the next day. And they won't even bring up the tongue lashing you gave them to the hounds in the media the previous hour. We all get it around here. The public doesn't and that's fine with everyone. In fact, that's the point."

"I suppose so. I guess I still have a shred of idealism left in me."

"A few more terms and that will fade," Fran said, smiling.

Madison laughed again.

"Speaking of which, I'm taking my granddaughters to President Wilson's fundraiser concert tonight at the Lincoln Theater. They are big *Bailee* fanatics. I don't know much about her but when they heard she was performing, they begged me for tickets."

"You're going to a fundraiser for the president?" Madison replied. "A Republican at a fundraiser for a Democratic president?" Madison's jaw dropped.

"It's a closed event with no press," Fran said swatting the air with a *who cares* gesture. "And like I said, behind closed doors, it's all relative. But I was just curious if you were going. I'd love to find a bar somewhere to get away from what will sound like screeching to me while my granddaughters teeny-bop through the night. I'd be happy to continue this discussion if you're going."

The two stopped where the hallway ended. Their offices were in opposite directions. "No, they invited me but I will pass," Madison said. "I can't believe the president is having a fundraiser right after a horrific terrorist attack. It doesn't seem right."

"Perhaps not," Fran replied adjusting her scarf. "But something terrible is always happening in the world. And political events take months of planning and can't change on a dime. Besides, if it were a Republican president the press would eat him alive. But let's face it, they are more than happy to give Wilson a free pass."

"That I agree with," Madison replied with a smile as the two said their goodbyes and returned to their respective offices.

CHAPTER 10

THE OPERATIVE CODE-NAMED ADDER PUT THE tray table up and removed his headphones as the flight attendant instructed. He gazed out the window over the city as the plane descended. Vienna was still the same as every one of his visits but this time it seemed like a gray haze had fallen over the streets and buildings. Adder sighed and rubbed his face. Today his hair and beard were dark black. His clothes were drab and unassuming. The quiet way about him ensured no one even thought to ask him questions. That was precisely his intention.

Adder disembarked and made his way to customs. He nonchalantly checked his passport to confirm which identity he was using today. Under normal circumstances, this would not have been necessary, but the drink had numbed his mind ever so slightly.

He gave a little smile to the customs agent, a pretty young Austrian who looked miserable in her job, as she studied his passport. She barely batted an eye before stamping and passing it back to Adder in a singular motion. She waved him off like an annoying school boy. For an instant, Adder had wished she would have caused trouble. Maybe then he would get caught and this whole thing would blow up before it began. But he was not so lucky. He never was. There were countless missions where he wondered if the end was near, perhaps even wanting it, but his training and pride, what little there was left, kept him going. He was a professional.

Trying to hide his annoyance, Adder waited for his suitcase for almost thirty minutes at the conveyor belt. There
was nothing of use in the bag. He only packed it because
traveling without one would have aroused suspicion. Even
if he secretly desired capture sometimes, the last thing he
wanted was to become an airport security success story for
young recruits at orientation. Tales of the heroic baggage
checker who stopped an international conspiracy, saved
hundreds of lives, and all for the good of the cause. No,
Adder would not be propped to distract these mundane
workers in their thankless industry. If he went down then
such an anticlimactic ending would be regretful.

He hunted down a bus headed to the center of the city.
Adder never took cabs. It was hard to blend into the scene
when it is just you and a driver. In Austria the cab drivers
were especially verbose, and he was in no mood for chit-
chat. Small talk could get you killed. So he took a bus to
melt into a sea of a people in unextraordinary fashion. The
ride was long and uncomfortable but Adder kept his head
down and away from prying eyes.

The bus pulled into the *Helferstorferstr* bus station and
Adder dashed off with his bag. It was a few blocks to his
hotel, and he caroused like a tourist, stopping for pictures
of architecture here and there. For this trip, he chose the
Hotel de France Wien. When you pay for sophistication,
privacy is a mandatory amenity. A seedy hotel had too
many low-lives. A hostel was an unnecessary gamble. Too
many odd people snapping photographs and getting in
your business. Besides, he would not share a room with a
pretentious college student backpacking through Europe.
A private room was hardly that in most establishments.

Check-in was painless. They asked few questions and
scurried him to his room in no time. The view from the

main window was breathtaking. It was a pity he had to pull the curtains closed with no intention of opening them again. He plopped his bag on his bed, opened it, and pulled out his jogging suit and a pair of worn tennis shoes. He changed, stretched his hamstrings, put on headphones, and made his way down the back stairs to the street exit.

Adder jogged in place for a minute while he surveyed both directions. He removed a piece of gum from his pocket, put it in his mouth, then headed East on Schottenring. After a few blocks he turned right on Servitengasse toward Hermann-Gmeiner Park. He ran a few circles around the kids play park and over the bridge overlooking the river and down the wooded bank.

Adder had hardly worked up a sweat when he reached the Blumensalon Ilse Böse florist. He jogged behind the building to an unassuming alley. Then he stopped running, jogged in place, and checked his pulse while he surveyed the area. With no one in sight he pulled a key from his pocket and approached a door that appeared to be part of one of the shops. He unlocked the door to a poorly lit staircase. Adder quickly entered and shut the door behind him. There were ten steps to the bottom. He squatted to examine a piece of dried gum on the bottom level door. If it had been cracked, then he knew someone had visited and the mission would be aborted. With the gum intact, he chipped it off with his finger and removed the panel underneath the doorknob to reveal a keypad where he punched an eight-digit code to gain entrance.

The room was pitch black. There were no windows, and it smelled damp. He flipped the lights on from a switch to the left of the doorway. The lights flickered as they gained power to reveal three tables in the middle of the room. Adder glided to each table to inspect the neatly organized equipment.

He had memorized the inventory: fifteen M27 Infantry Automatic Rifles, forty-five standard 30-round STANAG magazines fully loaded, thirty ET-MP grenades, fifteen Interceptor Multi-Threat Body Armor Systems, fifteen trench coats of differing colors, and thirty XM84 diversionary stun grenades. Four suicide vests with C-4 explosives were also ready for prime time. Standard communication equipment was charged.

Adder examined each piece of equipment. He surveyed the rifles, taking time to take a few apart to check the cleanliness. They were modern and effective. It had taken skill to get these into the country but the *dark web* was quite a resource these days.

When he rated his inspection satisfactory, he pulled his right pant leg up and removed an envelope taped to his leg. Inside the dossier were guard schedules, security protocols, and psychological research on security personnel and officials at the target. He placed the envelope on the table next to the hand grenades. He pulled an analog cell phone from his other pocket and left that on top of the envelope. Adder checked everything one more time before leaving.

He replaced the gum on the door with a fresh piece from his mouth, locked the door, and made his way back to the street. Adder placed the key underneath a broken lamp on the side of the wall next to the street-level door. He jogged back toward his hotel.

Adder briefly deviated from his run to stop and purchase a bottle of whisky. When he returned to his hotel, he walked back up the backstairs and entered his room. He locked the door and got a shower. After he dried off, he sat on his bed and took the bottle in his hand. Staring and shaking he said, "Dammit, I should have bought two."

Adder cracked open the cap, took a heavy swig, grimaced, and stared at the bottle once again.

Then, Adder wept like a baby. This was becoming a common occurrence.

CHAPTER 11

JASON PHILLIPS HAD LITTLE APPETITE AS he sat across from Peter Baylor at the Alibi restaurant in downtown DC. That did not prevent Peter from wolfing down a bowl of fish chowder and some sausage rolls. Jason poked at his Caesar salad nervously, hoping his apprehension would go unnoticed.

"Mm-hm" Peter grumbled as he slurped down the last bit of chowder and wiped his face with his napkin. "That's what I needed."

"I think you missed a drop," Jason said with disdain. Peter returned his barb with an awkward grimace.

Jason dropped his fork and crossed his hands over his lap. *Let's get this over with* he thought to himself.

"Thanks again for meeting with me," Peter said. "I wanted to make sure we're on the same page because I am looking to announce my candidacy this week, maybe next. Madison needs to be on my team now to make my announcement pop right out of the gate."

"Right," Jason replied.

Peter gave him a rigid look. "I have a solid fundraising network in place. I contacted Boyd's top donors and most of them are on board. Our first fundraising will leave every other challenger in the dust. I even have Boyd's general consultant and his digital team signed on for the primary. I'm ready to rock and there will be a lot of buzz pulling on emotional ties about Boyd's death and me being his right-hand man and whatnot. It will play well with Independents and low-information-voters. We'll get Democrats voting on emotion instead of policy, which is the only way to get them out to vote, anyway. We'll demonize whoever the Republican schlub is they put up as the end-all-be-all political villain that will take away women's right to vote or something. That should play well in Virginia."

"Of course," Jason said with casual coolness. "It sounds like you're well on your way. I suppose I just don't understand why you need Madison in all of this."

Peter shook his head and winced like someone jabbed him in the ribs. "Come on," he raised his voice. "Everyone knows how close Madison and Boyd were. It has to look like she's supporting me to honor his legacy. I must appear as the only choice; an anointment if you will. She is the Pope and I'm the bloody Holy Roman Emperor. This all has to play like my election is a formality, not an actual race. We don't want voters thinking too hard."

Jason could not look Peter in the eye. He knew that gave him away but he could not help it. Instead he cleared his throat. Most in DC shared Peter's cynicism but there was still a shred of idealism in Jason. Maybe he had not been on Capitol Hill long enough to strip away all his morality. Perhaps Madison's energy and commitment kept him honest. Whatever it was, it gave him strength for what he was about to say. But he had to perform the dance first.

"So tell me about your platform," he said after a long pause.

"Who cares?" Peter responded. "I told you my basic campaign strategy. No one will care about policy."

"Madison cares."

"Oh for Pete's sake, Jason… All right, fine. If that's what it takes. If you must know I will center my talking points on the oil spill in the Gulf. There isn't anything hotter in the news and people are pissed. Our most recent polling shows a shift in who people are blaming. At first, they were scared and angry at the terrorists. But now we're getting close to a month with the spill still out of control and polluting the ocean. Voters want blood from the oil companies. It has helped that the president has shown them no love and questioned their cleanup capabilities. I will hit on the fact that none of them had a plan in place to deal with this eventuality."

"You mean the terrorist attack?" Jason interjected. "Why would they ever have that on their radar? There has never been any credible threats against oil derricks. This is a brave new world we're living in and no one knows the rules anymore."

Peter looked at Jason like he had two heads. "That's not the damn point and you know it."

Jason threw his hands up and huffed.

"Listen," Peter said with elevated force. "You should know how to play this game by now. There is more than one way to win an election but the best way, and I do mean the best way, is to use world events to your advantage. If the economy takes a turn, you blame the incumbent for ignorant economic policies. If there is a crisis that costs lives, you make your opponent look weak and incapable of answering that 3:00 a.m. phone call. And if there's an oil spill and you can't find the responsible party, then you attack the people you can find—Big Oil."

"I guess, but it still seems a little crass," Jason said sheepishly.

"Well it is! No one said politics is tasteful. We have to dumb down the issue so the average Joe-sixpack can understand it in the simplest way possible. Those oil derricks would not have exploded if they had never been there in the first place. I will hit offshore drilling hard and call for a moratorium on new permits. We're going to create so much red tape it will make Big Oil's head spin."

"Yea, but that will not stop the Chinese or the Russians from drilling in international waters. That's where these attacks took place anyway."

Peter gave him the same perplexed look he did a minute ago. He felt like he was talking to a kindergartner and it showed.

"Perception is reality in politics," he replied in as calm of a voice as he could muster. "We can't do anything about the Chinese, the Russians, or if aliens want to build an oil derrick. So we focus on what we can control."

"Okay, okay, I get it." Jason's annoyance oozed. "So what else?"

"What do you mean?"

"What other policies are you running on?"

"Well, that's about it. I'd like to see an increase in the federal gas tax and a new carbon tax on big businesses… put that money into healthcare or something."

"You can't be serious? The beltway bandits and industry types in Northern Virginia will revolt."

"Well, yeah," Peter replied rolling his eyes again. "I will push for it when I'm in office but that's not going to be a cornerstone of my campaign. Populism is the order of the day."

"At least we can agree on that being an effective campaign strategy." Jason sighed. He resisted the urge to pull out his cellphone and fool around with anything but this vapid conversation. Another few minutes and he would have to leave or throw up.

"It is," Peter said as he folded his arms and peered down his nose. "So now will Madison be a *Baylor Burner* or what?"

"I'm sorry?"

"That's what we are calling my supporters. We'll let the pompous journalists take the credit and make it look like I have real grassroots energy. I think it has a nice ring to it."

"Yeah," Jason said. He was not sure if he had rolled his eyes.

Peter stared.

"Madison is more than willing to support the Democrat who wins the nomination for this senate seat," he said, trying to hide his glee. He had barely been able to contain himself waiting to deliver this line.

"Are you kidding me?" Peter said in a lowered voice as he hunched down close to the table. "I don't need her help in the general. It's Virginia, not Oklahoma. This seat is a slam dunk for Democrats. That's why I'm looking at four or five challengers. The real race is in the primary. And you and Madison know that!"

"The Congresswoman has no desire to get involved in a primary fight. Truth be told, she would prefer to sit the whole thing out. Boyd meant a lot to her and it sickens her to think about inserting herself into a fight over the scraps he left behind."

"Scraps?" Peter's face turned bright red like a disciplined child. "Virginia gets bluer every year. No Democrat will lose this seat for twenty years or more. This is a big game. There is no time to sit on the sidelines... Wait... Is she thinking about running?" Peter's eyes widened.

Jason jolted back in his seat. "What? No, come on now. I have had no conversation with her about that."

"I see what's going on here." Peter nodded his head. "She wants to play the emotional card as the heir apparent and snatch up that seat for herself!"

"Peter, you're losing it, man. The Congresswoman hasn't even finished her first term. And quite frankly, she has no desire for higher office and never has."

Peter shook his head and stood, almost knocking his chair on the floor. He dug around in his back pocket for his wallet, pulled it out, and threw five twenties on the table.

"You better listen well," Peter said as his face grew redder. "Madison better not pull a fast one on me. I've waited too long for this and have paid my dues. I get the opportunity of a lifetime served up on a silver platter and no one will stop me. There are forces at work here that Madison better not trifle with. You need not be concerned about the specifics just know certain people are pulling strings behind the scenes and if she throws a wrench in their plans, there will be hell to pay!"

Peter stormed out. A few frowning restaurant goers gave him looks as the large man swiftly dashed through the crowded establishment.

Jason felt queasy after hearing him describe Boyd's suicide as the "opportunity of a lifetime." He ignored the barb about unseen forces as nothing more than an idle threat from a spoiled brat.

Later, he would reexamine that conversation with a more enlightened perspective.

CHAPTER 12

MADISON LINED UP HER SHOT. SHE gazed down the fairway, cracked her neck, and stared at the ball. She took a deep breath, pulled back, and crushed forward with her driver. The golf ball exploded off the club with a metallic ping before it sailed right down the middle.

"That's a hell of a golf shot," Fran Norris said as she leaned on her golf club with one hand and shielded her eyes with the other, following Madison's ball to its landing spot. Their caddies scurried ahead to read their next shots toward the green. Madison nodded in approval as she dropped her club to her side and turned to Fran and said, "I can live with that."

"I'll say. You're having a heck of a game."

"How could I not on such a beautiful course?"

Fran and Madison were just finishing a rather competitive game at Robert Trent Jones Golf Course. Every part of the course was in immaculate condition. The water from Lake Manassas shimmered like dancing nymphs. A soft breeze kept them cool while their caddies kept them honest.

As the two walked toward their next shot, Madison hesitated before asking, "Forgive me if this seems rude and I'm thankful for the invite but how do you justify the cost of being a member here? It must be exorbitant."

Fran chuckled and replied, "Oh, it is. No doubt about that. But the owner has more than enough members to pay the bills. He likes to have muckety-mucks like me and other DC type folks playing his course. So I can play whenever I want for free. It's a bragging point for him and helps justify a membership fee for others. People that wish they were bigwigs are more than happy to cough up tens of thousands of dollars a year to play at a course frequented by politicians. The president plays here from time to time. Do you think he would play here if he got a bill the taxpayer would surely pay?"

"That would not look good," Madison cringed. "But I would not put it past Wilson. He's always been a do-as-I-say-not-as-I-do kind of guy."

Fran burst into laughter.

"You don't care for him, do you?" she asked.

"Oh, I don't know."

"Yes, you do."

"I didn't support him in the primary. But there are issues I agree with him on and others I don't. It's just that sometimes I think he likes being president more than the actual work involved with being president. I'm not the type who blindly follows someone just because we share the same party."

"Well, good for you," Fran said as she stooped next to her ball and prepared to drive the green.

"That's fifty-three yards to the pin, ma'am," Fran's caddie explained. Fran had already forgotten his name. He faded into the background until needed. "The pin is on a slight back slope. You'll want to drop it about seven feet from the hole to get the right amount of a roll."

"Well, we'll see about that," she replied. In an instant, she thwacked her ball about fifteen yards past the tee and off to the right. "And that's why golf is more frustrating than politics," she said with a smirk.

Madison laughed. "Maybe it's difficult to concentrate when we have so much on our plate these days."

"You got that right. I think it is worse for women in power too. Our minds race between policy, family, politics, and other priorities. Everything is interconnected and interweaving. We have a much bigger picture than men who only seem capable of handling one thing at a time."

"I suppose so."

They strolled down the fairway toward Madison's ball. Fran gently put her hand on Madison's arm, turned to her, and said, "You know, I worry about my granddaughters and the world they're growing up in and if they'll be safe. We're burning up our resources so quickly. We live in scary times and need strong leadership to get us through. Working in Washington gets me down, it really does. Most people are more interested in playing the game than getting things done. It's the same old story with each new Congress and it will take something monumental before we see radical changes for the better."

"I feel the same way," Madison said and turned away. She could feel Fran staring at her, waiting for something more.

"I want you to have a bright future," Fran said. "You have what it takes to go far in this town, if you're willing to do your duty."

Madison turned to her with a perplexed look and said, "I am not sure what you mean."

"I..."

Before Fran could answer both Madison and Fran's cell phone rang.

"That's not a good sign," Madison said before answering. It was Jason.

"What's up?" she said.

"There has been another terrorist attack," Jason said frantically. "It should hit the news any minute."

"Okay, what do we know?"

"Armed men, a dozen or so. They stormed OPEC headquarters in Vienna, Austria. There are hostages and at least one person has been killed already."

Madison sighed. She felt powerless, angry, disappointed, and sad all at the same time.

"You better get back here," Jason said.

"And do what? Go to another meeting?"

"You can't be golfing while a terrorist attack is underway. You'll be crucified in the press."

Madison cringed. She looked up to see Fran heading toward the clubhouse.

"All right. I'll be back soon. Keep me updated."

CHAPTER 13

THE RAIN WAS A PERFECT COVER. The terrorists could not have planned a better day for the attack. The key to their plan was the element of surprise. Each operative wore a long raincoat to hide their equipment, body armor, and weapons. If it had not been raining, fifteen Arabic men milling around OPEC headquarters in trench coats may have looked suspicious to security personnel.

Each man circled the building until precisely 9:17 a.m. They wore their cellphones in a shirt pocket tight to their chests. Their synchronized alarms went off with a vibration so no one could hear the coordinated attack. As soon as each man felt the vibration they sprinted toward the OPEC entrance while removing their jackets and revealing their M27 Infantry Automatic Rifles. Each had ET-MP grenades and XM84 diversionary stun grenades on their belts. A few wore suicide vests with C-4 explosives wrapped around their chests. They placed communication equipment on their ears and Interceptor Multi-Threat Body Armor Systems on their bodies. This was no ragtag group of ideological terrorists. With military precision, they stormed the poorly guarded target.

Within seconds they overwhelmed the guards. Two Austrian policemen pulled handguns but were shot dead before raising them. The other two guards threw their hands in the air and fell to their knees as they were surrounded by gunmen who put them in handcuffs and smacked them with the butts of their guns.

Two terrorists broke off from the rest of the group to lock and barricade the front doors. They hunkered down behind the security kiosk and aimed their guns at the door while the other thirteen men ran upstairs in a single file line. With no needed direction or discussion six men broke toward the administrative and regular offices with their guns held high.

The staff working at their desks and milling around the water cooler were shocked after men burst in waving guns and yelling, "Get up, everyone get up and move together to the middle of the room."

Without thinking the staff moved quickly. Many were crying or hyperventilating. Anyone, man or woman, who moved too slowly was bludgeoned by a terrorist. One portly man fell and was rewarded with a kick to the stomach. His coworkers had to drag him to the middle of the room where the rest of the staff congregated. They were held at gunpoint by three of the attackers while the other three rounded up remaining stragglers in the offices that encompassed most of the second floor.

The other seven operatives went straight for the boardroom. They knocked down the door to find OPEC representatives sitting in chairs and tables in a semicircle. Behind the main tables sat support staff. Six men, three on each side, screamed "Hands up, hands up!" as they spread to cover everyone in the room. The final gunman strolled into the middle of the room amidst screams and gasps. He placed his gun on the floor and raised his hand in the air.

In a heavy Arabic accent the man said, "Quiet please, I will have quiet."

He waited until the fearful cries subsided to whimpers. He put his arms behind his back and walked up and down the conference room studying each member and nodding his head as members stood with their hands in the air.

"Well then." He motioned to a man who removed a bag from his back pocket and circulated the room. "Please put all electronic devices into the bag including cellphones, laptops, tablets, and watches. We will collect these items only once. If I find you with one after this time you will be shot. I can assure you this is a very serious situation and we are in no mood for games. If you follow our directions then, in time, you will be freed. If you do not, then you will die. None of us care about you or your life. You are a bargaining chip, nothing more. We do not need all of you to get what we want. In fact, we could execute most of you and still achieve our objective. So do not test our resolve. You are now my prisoner and these men are your jailers. Treat them with respect and you will live."

Fear overtook the room. Some delegates and aides were praying. Others were sobbing. Many in complete shock showed no outward emotion. Everything happened fast and the reality of the situation proved difficult to process.

The terrorists were in complete control and had dug in when the Bundespolizei, the Austrian Federal Police, arrived. They formed a perimeter around the building and blocked traffic and pedestrians for three city blocks. Gruppeninspektor Lukas Baeder arrived on scene to take charge of the situation. He exited his police car and walked to the makeshift police truck command center. Cops in tactical gear positioned themselves in buildings and vehicles around the scene. Officers directed Kommissärs and tactical agents to assignments while fending off media who had caught wind of the situation and were showing their knack for annoyance.

Baeder approached his officers as they acknowledged his presence with a nod. "What's the status?" he said in a thick Austrian accent.

One subordinate stepped up to reply, "Within the last thirty minutes an unknown group of men stormed OPEC headquarters. They have control of the entire building and have barricaded themselves. They are heavily armed. We are trying to make contact now."

"Okay, give me the phone," Baeder ordered. A nearby Kommissär heard the command and approached with a cellular phone. "This is patched in to their main line. Heat signatures show they are in the conference room. This will dial into there."

"Very good," Baeder said as he hit the call button.

"Hello," a thick Arabic voice answered on the other end.

"This is Gruppeninspektor Lukas Baeder of the Bundespolizei, who am I speaking with?"

"Call me Mohammad."

"Very well, Mohammad. We understand you are armed and have hostages. It is my job to make sure this comes to a peaceful conclusion."

"Quiet," Mohammad said. "We have no desire to hurt anyone. We view this as a simple transaction. If you cooperate, then we will surrender. We are all prepared to go to jail or die. Give us what we want and everyone can go home. We have harmed no one yet nor do we have plans to do so unless you provoke us. Any attempt at rescue will result in us blowing the building and everyone in it. Do not test our resolve or blood will be on your hands."

"Well, no one here wants that, sir. What are your demands?"

"We have several Shuhada' Alnnabi brothers-in-arms who have been falsely imprisoned for fighting for the prophet. They must be released into a country of our choosing as soon as possible. Once we have confirmed they are free, then we will give ourselves up."

"And who do you want freed?"

"I will provide a list. But there are seven being held in Guantanamo Bay, another five in Yemen, and fourteen in secret CIA prisons around the world. In the meantime you will show your good faith by not acting on any hostage protocols. I am well aware of your tactics and procedures. If anything happens, we will kill hostages. Understood?"

"Yes, but could we…"

Click. Mohammad hung up.

Baeder sighed.

The man who gave the Gruppeninspektor the initial report asked, "Should we cut the power and Internet, sir?"

"No!" Baeder said. "That will get someone killed. They know what they are doing and are expecting that. Their leader said they will surrender. That's a remarkable admission this early in the game. They must mean it. Let's stay back and wait for further instructions. I have a feeling this will be resolved sooner than anyone could expect."

"As you command."

In an adjacent room to where the hostages were held, one gunman was busy typing away on a computer. Two other gunmen were setting up the Shuhada' Alnnabi flag in front of a webcam. The leader, the man known as Mohammad, entered the room and said, "Are we ready to go?"

"Yes, sir. We are ready to record."

"And you are not connected to the Internet yet, correct? This is not a live broadcast."

"Of course, once we are done I will upload it to our network. As long as they don't block our signal we can get it out."

"I'm confident they will do no such thing. They are too stupid and weak. But even infidels like them will grow weary if this takes too long."

Mohammad retrieved a paper from his pocket. He had each member country listed in order of largest oil production.

"Let us start with the Secretary-General and then move on to Saudi delegates."

"Two gunmen exited the room only to reappear a minute later with the OPEC Secretary-General, a fifty-eight-year-old man from Nigeria. Fear prevented him from speaking coherently. Noticeably shaking, he was paraded in and placed in front of the webcam on his knees. He rocked back and force as he prayed with tears streaming down his face.

"We are recording in two seconds," the man behind the computer said. He pointed at Muhammad to indicate the recording had begun.

Mohammad stood behind the man and with a scowl said, "Today Shuhada' Alnnabi becomes a permanent member of OPEC. And our one-and-final act is to dismantle this cabal of infidel whores. Our lands are ravaged by greed and destroyed by these evildoers who seek excessive wealth to further break the backs of God's soldiers. Oil is a curse on our lands. It turns men into sinners as they turn their backs on the prophet. Allah has commanded the end of oil. It will no longer be a tool for sin. Shuhada' Alnnabi strikes a dagger in the hearts of this great Satan and will continue to fight until all oil production ceases. Today we martyr ourselves to show blood is thicker than oil. Allahu Akbar, Allahu Akbar."

A man off-screen handed Mohammad a scimitar. The Secretary-General could not stop blubbering as he protested. With a scream, Mohammad chopped his head clean off with one powerful blow. As the lifeless body dropped to the ground, the two terrorists in the room dragged the corpse off camera and threw it in a nearby closet.

With the recording still rolling they went into the conference room to retrieve the Saudi delegates.

Gruppeninspektor Baeder gave frantic orders as he stared at the front of OPEC headquarters. His snipers could not locate any targets and if they had, he would have ordered them to stand down anyway. Inside the windowed entrance he could see a barricade close to the steps. There was slight movement but not enough to see who was behind the barricade. For all he knew the terrorists planted hostages there in case the police stormed. Regardless, he had two teams ready to infiltrate at a moment's notice.

The vibration of his cellphone broke his concentration. He motioned to his officers to stand by while he answered.

"Hello?"

"Gruppeninspektor Baeder?"

"Yes."

"This is Jean from the European Union Agency for Network and Information Security, are you the commander running the hostage situation at OPEC headquarters?"

"Yes, what do you have for me?"

"Get to your command vehicle at once, I'm emailing you a link. There is a terrorist broadcast that claims to be coming from inside OPEC. It's just starting now."

"Can you shut it down?"

"We're working on it but we thought you should know right away."

"I'll call you back," he said running to his command vehicle. He pushed one of his men out of the way from a console while he logged into his email, found the link from Jean, and opened a browser. He saw a man in a suit on his knees while a terrorist held a sword behind him in front of the Shuhada' Alnnabi flag.

Baeder gasped as the sword came crashing down on the suited man's neck in gory fashion. He put his hand to his mouth then reached for his radio.

"Be prepared to storm, stand by," he radioed his teams. He grabbed his phone and dialed the number that came in from Jean at ENISA a few moments ago.

"My God," Jean said as he picked up.

"Can you confirm this is streaming from my location?"

"That's the thing, we…"

Before Jean could answer an explosion rocked the city block. Police and bystanders ducked for cover or were thrown to the ground from the force. Fire erupted from the top of OPEC headquarters. He could hear gunshots popping one at a time from inside the building.

He reached for his phone which had fallen to the ground from the explosion. "Jean, are you there?"

"Yes, and the video is still rolling."

"How is that possible?" Baeder screamed.

"It… It isn't live. It was a video uploaded to Jihadi websites fourteen minutes ago. Everything you're watching already happened."

"Oh, Jesus," Baeder whispered while he felt his eyes swelling with tears. Shaking his head, he grabbed the radio again, pressed the call button, and said "Storm!"

In an instant, two teams in single file poured toward the front of the building from behind police cars on opposing sides. The front two officers carried hard armor shields and men behind them each had their rifles pointed toward the door. The explosion destroyed the glass windows at the front of the entrance as they charged in without delay.

Sounds like firecrackers filtered the air as terrorists from behind the barricade opened fire. Three policemen took bullets and dropped as others fanned out, took cover, and returned fire. The sharpshooting policemen hit two gunmen before a third tried to run up the stairs. He was quickly shot in the leg and back before falling on the stairs, clutching his body in pain. The police teams swarmed the steps while one officer checked the man for weapons, pulled his arm behind his back and led him out of the building. Other police entered to pull out wounded officers. One of them was already dead while the other two tried to limp away.

The rest of the teams motioned forward up the steps. As soon as they reached the second floor, they witnessed pure disaster. The whole floor was on fire with walls collapsed or collapsing and bodies strewn everywhere. Thick black smoke permeated the room. The officer in the front choked on the smoke before signaling to get back. As they retreated down the steps, he glimpsed what must've been the conference room. There were headless bodies everywhere. No one stirred. They were all dead.

Later, police would confirm seventy-five delegates and support staff were murdered by fifteen terrorists. All but one either died from the explosions from suicide vests or had shot themselves as the building burned.

CHAPTER 14

JOHN CALLAHAN WATCHED THE NEWS OF the OPEC attack with a frazzled mind. His eyes darted from the TV to his computer with nervous regularity. On one browser tab, he monitored the ETF commodities heat map, which showed nothing but red for oil companies. In another, he watched the commodity prices of oil in real time skyrocket. With oil still gushing out in the Gulf of Mexico, combined with today's terror attack, many wallets were a bit lighter today.

John's cellphone rang. He glanced at the caller ID. It was one of his biggest clients, Jeremiah Hankins.

"Jeremiah, this is John, how are you, buddy?"

Jeremiah, wasting no time, replied gruffly, "What the hell is going on? This is not what we discussed." He breathed heavily on the phone as if he had just run five miles.

"I understand where you're coming from, I do. But there is no way I could have known terrorists would—"

Jeremiah cut him off. "My natural gas stocks are plummeting. My entire portfolio is based on production. Increased oil costs make production more expensive. Two of my top companies are already adjusting revenue forecasts and it's not looking good, John. What the hell am I supposed to do?"

"Listen, dramatic spikes are almost always temporary," John said, wiping the sweat from his forehead. "I realize there have been world events that have caused this but I'm recommending you stay the course."

The line went silent. John heard Jeremiah grind his teeth. "This is not a damn temporary spike! OPEC is in complete disarray. They lost some real leaders today. Their replacements will not be half as good. You don't get it, do you? OPEC relies on a few key individuals to keep the trains running. And now they're all dead. Their entire system is based on backroom deals and handshake agreements. It's the dark ages and a house of cards over there. It's all crumbling now."

John cleared his throat and fidgeted, rocking back and forth. "This is not a time to panic. We can get through this!" He did not realize he had raised his voice.

"No, no, no, no! You said fracking would keep oil constant no matter what, John. I realize two major terror attacks were impossible to predict, but you had me put too many eggs in one basket. I'm getting killed. Companies are going under. I have tons of money in trucking and manufacturing. Natural gas companies need oil to do business. And my portfolio is already down thirteen percent since last week. It's too much!"

"So what do you want me to do?" John threw his hand up in the air.

"Nothing, John, nothing. I'm moving to another broker. I'm looking to retire in a few years and I can't take this kind of hit. Sorry, goodbye."

John begged for Jeremiah to stay on the line but it was too late.

"Dammit!" he screamed.

John opened his email. Every subject line looked about the same. From "I'm out" to "What were you thinking?" this was the worst day of his career. He could not bring himself to examine his own portfolio.

The final bell rang as the NYSE closed for the day.

879 points gone. Futures would be worse. And there was nothing he could do. If he advised his clients to sell, then they'd lose big, and he had no real idea how to get it back. If he told nervous investors to stay the course, then he looked impotent and clueless.

John kicked his chair away with the back of his legs as he stood and paced back and forth. He scurried over to the bar in the basement and removed an unopened bottle of twenty-three-year Pappy Van Winkle. He cracked it open and poured a healthy dose into a nearby glass. He plopped down on the adjacent sofa and took a long snort. John sniffed as he took down the sweet whisky. Breathing deep, he turned off the TV and closed his eyes.

Then, he sobbed.

A few minutes passed and his cellphone rang again. "I can't do this anymore" he said to himself. He glanced at the caller ID, which said "blocked." John figured it was another irate client but hiding would do him no good. He was taking a beating today and tomorrow would be worse. But if he did not take his lumps then he would be finished. If he was not already.

"Hello," he said as he accepted the call.

...

"Oh, hi," he replied. "I did not expect to hear from you." John's voice wobbled with fear and surprise.

...

"Okay..."

...

He went quiet as he listened.

"That is quite a proposition, but..."

...

CHAPTER 15

THE NATIONAL MALL IN WASHINGTON, D.C., has witnessed many historical events. From civil rights speeches to Earth-shattering global policies hammered out on a park bench, there may be no place where so much has been put in motion to change the course of history. And it is also a place where opinions of every spectrum are on display.

On this warm summer day the attentions of the Mall-goers turned to a large wooden structure, assembled by volunteers and activists. Although not to scale as the original, this structure replicated Noah's Ark. Put together with particle board and some rusty nails, handmade signs floated in the wind on bedsheets and poster board flanking the boat-like creation. Some had simple messages like, "Ban Fracking!" or "Break Free From Fossil Fuels." While others were more direct and controversial like, "Death To Oil Companies" and "Save Mother Earth, Stop Breeding." A mishmash of broadly defined environmental groups was well-represented this day.

When the final wall of the Ark was erected, one of the event organizers spray painted, "Plan B When Global Warming Puts Us All Under Water." A boisterous cheer erupted from every section of the protest, from the drum circles to the impromptu poetry slams. A waft of herb and patchouli oil filled the air.

Demonstrations of this sort often go unnoticed on the National Mall. You would be hard-pressed to visit Washington, D.C., without seeing some protest. The commonality is as frequent as they are mundane. But this day was a rare opportunity for environmentalists. In a stage set up adjacent to the protest, with the makeshift Ark in the background, sat superstar news anchor Reginald Goldsmith. Before him stood his camera crew and members of his production team.

Goldsmith, a silver-haired forty-something was easy to spot in a crowd with his rigid jawline and commanding voice. But it was his demeanor and blunt interview style which made him the #1 newscaster on the planet. Televisions across Capitol Hill were always tuned to his program.

Goldsmith spent the last few minutes covering news of the day as well as segments concerning the Ark protest. His production team would later splice the highlights to air in prime time that night. Due to his gravitas, Goldsmith's current interviewee should have been nervous, but his youth and inexperience became more of an asset than a hindrance, as he failed to assess the gravity of the moment.

Face to face on stage with Goldsmith, one of the main organizers of the event, a smiley chap named Blaze was having the time of his life.

"So," Goldsmith began, "*Planet Rescue* has gone to great lengths to capitalize off the recent tragedies involving oil production. The terrorists attack on oil derricks in the Gulf of Mexico and at OPEC headquarters, to name the most pertinent. How do you respond to those who think you're just refusing to let a crisis go to waste?"

Blaze sniffed and smiled from ear to ear. In a dopey delivery he said, "Hey, I get it, man. We're fighting a battle for Mother Earth and our message has been the same for years. We have to do what we can to awaken the people, man. There's a war going on that is fueled by racism, sexism, white supremacy, and hatred of different people and it all comes back to oil and other fossil fuels. If we don't do something quick, then we're all going to be drowning from global warming. And if it takes one of those once-in-a-lifetime events to wake the people then that's the way it has to be... man."

Goldsmith blinked and cleared his throat. "Right..." he replied. Shuffling papers he crossed his hands, leaned back, and faced Blaze. "So, tell me, what is it you want to see done, specifically?"

"I'm really glad you asked that, man," Blaze replied with a smirk. "It's time that the politicians in DC acted. They have built their stock portfolios off the backs of greed and Big Oil and now it's time for the people to take back the power. We want to see the end of fracking and all other oil production all over the world. The government should go 100 percent renewable energy and then go to the United Nations and pass a law that says the world needs to do the same thing. That would be a big-time start."

"You understand the UN doesn't pass laws, right?"

Blaze's head cocked to the side like a perplexed dog. "You're missing the point."

Reginald raised an eyebrow. "Okay, enlighten me."

"I will—that's what I do. It's time to start the conversation. You're already seeing governments in Canada and Europe pushing to stop dependence on Big Oil. But here in America, the blood money that Big Oil uses to grease up politicians is too much. If we stop using oil, they stop getting their money, and our politicians will do the right thing once the money stops. Don't you see?"

Goldsmith coughed and pushed his notes away. "Your heart is in the right place. You're rightfully concerned about the environment and you want to do something. You and your organization have done a good job of getting people who care about your cause together in the same place. And as to your motivations, I'm with you. We probably disagree on several policy positions, if you could ever hammer those out we'd be sure, but there is a need for change on several levels."

Blaze gyrated his hands in a pointing motion at Goldsmith, smiled, and said, "Yeah, you get it!"

"Right. But let's get serious for a moment. Where do you go from here to accomplish your mission?"

"Exactly, yeah. We are launching nationwide protests in locations all over the nation and stuff. Our followers will show Big Oil fat cats we mean business. We're going to coal plants, fracking sites, oil company headquarters and offices and we're going to be loud and we're going to get the people behind us. They're going to learn that global warming is killing us and we won't stop until something is done."

Reginald sat back and crossed his arms. "Well, good luck with that, Mr. Blaze. I hope we can chat again."

"Most definitely, man."

Goldsmith turned to face the camera and said, "Well that was something. Say what you will but the emotion is real. These young adults care about the planet and they want something done. As to how that happens exactly, that remains to be seen. But hopefully my next guest will shed light on just that. Joining me after this commercial break is the always colorful Representative Madison Gladstone from the great state of Virginia."

As the camera turned off Jason Phillips pulled his Prius to the curb in an adjoining street. Madison pulled down the vanity mirror in the passenger seat and inspected her makeup. Jason tapped his fingers on the steering wheel.

Without breaking her concentration, Madison said, "You told him I'm not talking about Boyd or his suicide, right?"

"Of course," Jason replied. "I mentioned it to his producers at least three times. They said it would not be brought up. But…"

"But, what?"

"You know."

"Yeah." Madison shook her head. She knew she had to be prepared for anything. TV personalities and reporters are like toddlers desperate for attention, eager to please themselves while forsaking all others in the process.

Jason watched the Ark protest and sneered. "That's quite a demonstration, isn't it?"

Madison put her lip gloss down and moved her head from side to side in the mirror. She smacked her lips and said, "Their heart is in the right place, not that it will accomplish anything. Protests never do."

"Good Lord, Congresswoman, don't say that in your interview! Besides, the fact that Reginald Goldsmith is here makes a difference. People pay attention to him. He can move mountains with public relations, and—"

"Didn't I tell you not to be so star-struck?" Madison interrupted.

Jason laughed. "Well, good luck. I'll try to find a parking spot but it's not likely. I'll swing around the block a few times until you're done."

Madison gave him a thumbs up as she exited the car. Goldsmith's producers headed her way in a frenzy. They attached a microphone in stride and peppered her with last-minute details. Anyone in public life always had two personalities: one for the rolling cameras and one for every other time. Madison played this game since the height of her father's political career. She waltzed to the seat on the stage previously occupied by Planet Rescue's eloquent spokesperson and sat, smoothed her dress, and cleared her throat.

Reginald Goldsmith was furiously writing notes and failed to acknowledge her presence for a good minute before saying, "It's so good to have you, Madison. I'm looking forward to this," without looking up. Madison just smiled.

"All right, Reggie," a producer said, "You good?" Reginald cracked his neck and knuckles, cleared his throat, and moved his jaw up and down, and back and forth.

"Let's do it. Madison, you ready?"

"Yeppers," she said, trying to hide her disdain at Goldsmith's radiating arrogance.

"Okay," the producer said, "5, 4, 3..." then she mouthed the final numbers as the camera light turned red.

"Thank you for staying with us during our commercial break," Goldsmith began. "I'm here with one of the most recognizable faces of the newest congressional class. Representative Madison Goldstone from the great state of Virginia is with us, Madison, welcome and thank you for being here on this glorious day on the National Mall."

Madison smiled. She was calm, relaxed, and comfortable. She was right at home in front of a camera even if she despised it. "Happy to be here."

"So let's jump right into it," Goldsmith said turning to face her, "Planet Rescue today kicked off a nationwide protest against oil companies in their quest to promote renewable energy. In a twist of fate, the recent terrorist attacks have shifted the global conversation towards energy policy. Do you feel that's an appropriate conclusion for public debate or are we taking our eye off the ball with concerns to radicalism?"

"That's a fair point, Reginald. And thank you for having me, I'm always glad to witness democracy in action like we're seeing today in DC. But we, as a nation, and the federal government, as a lawmaking body, are perfectly able to walk and chew gum at the same time. I have the utmost confidence in our law enforcement and military to bring these killers to justice, regardless of the national conversation. As an elected official I have a duty to always look at the long game and energy policy is important."

"Do you believe the protests like the one here today are missing the point regarding global terrorism?" Goldsmith asked.

"No, I don't think so. Americans have the God-given right to express themselves. There is much injustice in the world and just because you don't address it all at the same time doesn't make you wrong or belittle your point."

"Fair enough," Goldsmith said as he glanced at his notes. "But in terms of actual policy will anything happen and if so, what? Too often national outrage is short-lived, and it does not last long enough for Congress to get moving."

Madison laughed. Goldsmith gave a surprised expression. "I'll be the first to admit that Congress is inefficient," Madison smiled. "There's no doubt about that. But here's the thing, there will always be a need for new energy solutions. That's why clean, renewable, and cheap sources of energy are important. And this is a bipartisan issue. The problem is neither side of the aisle can analyze it from a nonpartisan perspective."

Reginald's face cocked to one side. "Can you elaborate?"

"On one side you have those who say global warming will result in the end of civilization. On the other, you have skeptics who argue data is not conclusive enough to launch major policy initiatives that may cripple the economy. But there is a middle way. We don't need unnecessary government regulation. Instead we need the free market to do its job. The company that produces a vehicle not reliant on fossil fuels will corner the market. The person who invents a way to stop carbon dioxide from flooding our atmosphere from factories and plants will change the world. Innovation is the key to solving this problem, not rules and guidelines."

"That's an interesting concept," Reginald said. His voice was monotone. "I'd like to delve more into that but our time is short. If I could I'd like to turn to the oil spills in the Gulf of Mexico, which are still raging. Even in the face of terrorist threats President Wilson has focused almost entirely on stopping this spill with no positive result. His latest idea is to drop golf balls into the holes and use a machine, which boasts investment from an A-List Hollywood actor, to clean affected water. Is Wilson just grasping at straws here?"

Madison crossed her legs. "Well, I support the president in his efforts to stop what is perhaps the greatest environmental calamity of our time. And there is no playbook to follow here. We have to get creative with solutions. The oil companies are working overtime to entertain ideas and the president will try anything. That is commendable."

"Well, we shall see," Reginald said dryly. "Now before we go, I wanted to discuss one more thing. Senator Radford was a close friend of yours and a mentor. His death rattled us all." He paused for effect, leaned in, and asked, "How are you doing?"

Goldsmith grabbed her hand in an overt effort to console her. Madison's jaw dropped as she grimaced looking at his hand, then pulled it back. Goldsmith was startled. Madison squinted her eyes and shook her head.

"I'm devastated. How the heck am I supposed to feel?"

They stared at each other before Goldsmith said, "Well, thank you again for joining us."

The cameras stopped rolling.

CHAPTER 16

BACK IN HER OFFICE, MADISON PULLED the shades down and rubbed her temples. With closed eyes she attempted to concentrate on anything other than politics. At this stage of the game she should have been immune to the conceit of the players. Everyone was in it for themselves, that much was known, but the intricate details of succeeding in politics and the surrounding industry was truly an art form. She may have embarrassed Reginald Goldsmith and the video clip of her snapping would surely recirculate through social media for the rest of the news cycle. His ratings would increase and she would earn some new fans and more than a few haters.

Madison shook her head. It had been quiet for almost five minutes. She wondered if that was a record. Madison pondered whether she could do this job for long. Recently a two-year term in the House of Representatives seemed so short. Now though, it was an eternity. She sighed and took a deep breath before hearing a knock at the door.

"That didn't last long," she said to herself. "What?" she yelled.

The door opened. Madison did not bother to turn around, expecting Jason to enter. Then, in a commanding voice, she heard, "I'm not interrupting anything am I?"

Madison twisted to see Special Agent Walter Robinson.

"You caught me off guard," she said.

"I doubt that happens often."

"I suppose. But you seem to be pretty good at it," she said in as rigid a voice as she could muster. Madison motioned for him to sit down.

"Truth be told," Madison said, "I expected my chief of staff."

"Yeah," Walter replied, "He's shell-shocked; looks like someone may have given him a tongue lashing or the silent treatment."

Madison blushed. She fidgeted with various items on her desk. Hoping her distraction techniques worked, she threw her hands in the air. "Yes, well, that's politics for you." She made a mental note to speak with Jason about the interview. He did the best he could to tell Goldsmith's producers she did not want to discuss Boyd's death. They lied, as the media often does. He even warned her. It was not his fault.

"Look," Robinson started as he sat, "Last time we chatted was awkward. I didn't mean to blindside or offend you. May I be frank?"

"Please, do."

"This job has its trials as I'm sure you can imagine. I have spent a lot of time trying to get into the world of a public servant who took his own life. It's not the thing you dream about as a kid. But it has to be done because that's the job. We have a duty to get answers if we can and there is little room for etiquette. Sometimes, I feel like I'm losing my humanity. Everyone else involved can and should mourn the death of this man. You grieve, you honor his legacy, and you move on for your sanity because humans are necessarily resilient. But as much as I'd like to, I can't leave it at that. I have to poke and prod until it reaches some conclusion. I didn't know Senator Radford when he was alive. But looking into the things he did, I wish I had.

And while his death haunts me, it motivates me to keep me going. This job, it is difficult, and sometimes I wonder if I have the mental toughness to keep going. That may translate into coming across as cold or insensitive. But it does not mean I'm trying to make things difficult, I want the truth."

Madison was speechless, a rarity for a politician. Robinson beheld her with soft blue eyes like an old friend instead of an FBI agent.

"Where are you from, Agent Robinson?"

"Call me Walter." He smiled.

"Okay, Walter." Madison smiled back.

"I grew up in Omaha. After college, I joined the police force. I was a beat cop for years before moving to homicide… cracked a few high-profile cases there that got the attention of the local FBI field office. Before I realized it, I was in the Academy and have not looked back since."

"The FBI must take up a lot of your time I imagine," Madison said in a more concerned tone than intended.

"Yeah, it doesn't do well for a personal life I'll admit. But now and again there's an opportunity to do something worthwhile."

"Like finding out why a senator took his own life?"

"Maybe."

They both looked off to the side for a moment. Madison rested her head in her hand, slumped, and then asked, "I appreciate the apology. If it helps, your humanity is just fine. And I can relate. We're both in jobs that often require sacrifices most would never consider making."

"You got that right," Walter said with a smirk.

"If you have any other questions for me, I'm happy to do what I can."

"Well, that's not why I came here today. Truthfully, I shouldn't be here."

Madison sat up. "Why not?"

"I wanted to update you on facts of the case. I shouldn't be doing that though. From a procedural point of view there's no reason. In the FBI, procedure is like Gospel. But the beat cop in me says sometimes the rules need to be bent."

"And now is one of those times?" Madison sounded surprised.

"Perhaps. I trust you'll keep this confidential, right?"

"Of course."

"On Senator Radford's computer screen he had a web browser opened to a personal email account. Records show it was created a week prior to his death. Not a single email was received nor had any been sent. But there was one email in the drafts. In the covert world this is how many nefarious characters communicate. Emails are so easily intercepted and read, if I told you specifics, you'd never send one again. But if multiple parties keep login information for an account, they can check the drafts for messages, read them, then delete them without ever sending it to anyone. There is no real record it ever happened and it cannot be intercepted."

"Who was it addressed to?" Madison found herself engrossed. Boyd was no man of international mystery. He was as close to a straight shooter as she could imagine. This was getting weirder by the minute.

"No one. And the subject line was blank. So we don't have a lot to go on at this point in time."

"What was in the email?"

"Not much. It was only a few lines. But, it was about you."

Madison's eyes bulged. "About me, what about me?"

"He said he was doing what he was doing to protect you."

"Oh my God…" Madison held her stomach as if she was going to be sick. She stood and relocated to the corner of her office, turned, and faced Walter with concern in her eyes.

"Let me rephrase that. He was not blaming you for his death. In fact, he did not even stipulate that 'what he was doing' involved his suicide. But it seems likely that he was trying to protect you from something. And not only that, he led us down this path by leaving that window open with no effort to hide this email account."

Madison rubbed her temples again. "I don't know what to say. Is that it, did he say anything else?"

"Yea, there was a warning."

"Warning for what?"

"He said you were to be left alone. Something to the effect of it was not right treating you like a pawn and it sickened him that he ever had anything to do with it."

"Wait, what does that mean? Boyd involved me in something, put me in danger somehow?" Madison paced between her desk and the corner of her office. Everyone has secrets on Capitol Hill. She was not naïve enough to think Boyd did not have a few skeletons in his closet. But, this was too much.

"That's what I'm trying to find out and why this investigation is still open."

Madison fought back tears. She lost a part of herself the day Boyd died. Every time she spoke of him it brought her back to the pain she felt the moment she was informed of his death. "He brought none of this up before. You have to believe me."

"I do. But I also theorize the senator was wrapped up in something big. I can only speculate. However, all of his files and correspondence on his computer were erased. Congressional computers document everything in case of FOIA requests. Somebody wiped his computer clean. There is nothing there, no backups, and we can find no other records on the congressional server."

Madison braced. A dark thought pervaded her mind. She did not want to know, not really, but she had to ask. "Is it possible he was murdered?"

Robinson paused and stared at Madison as he gathered his thoughts. Madison was distressed and he was not making the situation more tolerable. "No, there is no doubt that he killed himself."

An overwhelming feeling of guilt swept Madison for sensing a tinge of relief. When compared to the possibility of murder she was morbidly glad it had been suicide.

"There's one more thing," Robinson said. Madison braced herself. "I'm getting pressure to drop the case."

"*What*? From who?" Madison pounded her desk with her fist.

Walter leaned back and adjusted his cuff links. "My superiors hinted at it recently. Now, they're trying to move me on to other cases and want final reports. They act as if it's just a bureaucratic process, finish the job, and move on to the next. But something is off. I can't let this go."

"If you need me to do anything—If I can do something, you'll tell me, right?"

"Absolutely." Walter nodded his head. "I will keep going as long as I can. There is a reason the senator did this and I will find out why. Other than the draft email, there were no suicide note, no financial problems, or infidelities as far as I can tell. His staff and family all said he was one of the few genuine people on the Hill who held the same persona whether at a campaign event or behind closed doors."

"He did," Madison said. "I'll see if there is something maybe I missed. I'll try to do some digging."

"That would be great. I'll keep you updated best I can."

"Thank you."

Walter stood and made for the door. Madison gazed at her desk, lost, before Walter turned and said, "There's one thing I wanted to ask you if you don't mind."

"Of course not."

"What do you know of Peter Baylor, Senator Radford's chief of staff?

"He's an opportunistic little shit."

Walter laughed. "Yeah, I get that impression too."

"Could he be involved?"

"I have no specific reason to believe he would be involved. He rubbed me the wrong way when I questioned him. He was nervous. I am checking him out. But again, please keep this between us."

"Absolutely," Madison said. They nodded to each other as Walter left.

Madison glanced at her cellphone. The *Newscycle* with Reginald Goldsmith broadcast was about to air. It seemed trivial at this point but she wondered if they would edit out the part where she snapped. Not likely, but there was a chance.

She turned on her television to see the face of the pop singer, Bailee. She was sitting next to her rapper husband, Kronik. At the bottom of the screen was an 800 number. Madison had seen this commercial so many times she had it memorized.

"We both stand behind President Wilson in his efforts to stop the horrific oil spill in the Gulf of Mexico," Bailee said. "But he needs your help. Please call right away to make a donation to help with the cleanup process. Fish, birds, and other wildlife have been decimated by the oil. You can make a difference with even the smallest donation. Thank you."

The commercial ended as Reginald Goldsmith's face filled the screen.

"Here we go," Madison said to herself. *I should be nervous*, Madison thought. But her mind drifted elsewhere.

CHAPTER 17

THE MAN WITH THE CODENAME ADDER could not help but reflect on his many disturbing memories as he looked in the mirror of his old, smelly, stolen passenger van. Adder was old enough to remember the 1970s protests and he recalled more color to the traditional hippie outfit. These days the protest uniform was much drabber, but the slogans were more creative.

He wore a black t-shirt with the words "Greed Kills" in white lettering emblazoned across his chest. His ripped jeans were soiled and used. He wore long black hair extensions with a streak of purple dyed in the front. On the passenger side seat was a Guy Fawkes mask. Adder tried not to laugh at the sight of his ridiculous costume while zipping up a tattered blue hoodie and exiting the van.

On each side of the *Planet Rescue* camp sat raggedy tents as protesters in similar garb milled around. The distinct aroma of marijuana lingered in the air. Homeless wanderers mixed with college students on summer vacation. The camp burst at the seams as occupiers filled every inch of the state-owned monument grounds in this little Pennsylvania town. At the center stood a pointy monument dedicated to soldiers lost in Vietnam that Adder was sure no one at the camp recognized. A young man appearing fresh from high school was ranting on a megaphone as the crowd congregated.

"And we will take the fight to the polluters," he railed to sounds of hollering and applause. "No longer will Big

Oil determine the future. It is up to us to shut them down for good! Big Oil continues to rape our land and force us dependency on their greed. Yeah!"

The man raised his fist in the air to another round of yelling and chanting. Adder perused the crowd and spotted one of the few women in attendance. The girl must have been twenty-something but was relatively clean compared to the grubby crowd. Over disheveled dreadlocks emblazoned in rhinestones her headband read, "I am the 99%." Her salmon colored hoodie was zipped tight and her black pants were more tattered than Adder's. The girl hung on every word of the speaker. Her eyes were deep blue and moist from tough talk exploring environmental issues and crimes against humanity perpetrated by oil companies. Adder could not help but smile as he moved in her direction.

The speaker did not have much of a conclusion. He stopped talking at some point and everyone in the camp went about their business. Adder slid right behind the girl as she turned. They locked eyes.

"This better not be another bullshit pep talk," he said. The girl gave a perplexed look and replied, "What do you mean?"

"Never mind. Don't worry."

Adder turned and marched back toward his van.

"Hey, wait up," the girl called as she jogged to catch up. Adder suppressed a grin.

The girl grabbed his arm, stopping him cold. Adder sneered at the ground and shook his head. "What's wrong?" she asked. "You didn't like the protest plan?"

"There were not a lot of plans discussed," Adder said. "There was a lot of talk and little action."

She blinked and scowled.

"You're young and I'm glad people like you are involved. But, trust me; I've been around for a long time. Back in the seventies we did the same thing and it got us nowhere. Oil companies are still destroying the planet, are as greedy, and as big as ever."

"That doesn't mean surrender is an option," she said impishly.

Guitar strumming echoed throughout the camp. The orange glow of the sun filtered through the trees as it began to set. Adder and the girl strolled side by side, passing a range of people fit for a circus.

"What's your name?" Adder asked.

"Daisy."

"That's beautiful. I bet you had hippie parents?"

Daisy blushed. "My dad ran out before I was born. My mom was big in the protests against Vietnam though."

This is just too damn perfect, Adder thought. "I knew it. You've got her spirit."

Daisy blushed harder.

"I'm Jonas," Adder said. "I bet me and your mom would have a lot in common. We were probably at a lot of those same protests. I spent most of my time in Berkeley and San Francisco in those days."

Daisy's eyes lit up. "That was at the heart of the movement!"

"Yup," Adder said with a smile. "But it wasn't enough for me. I wanted real change and I would have been damned otherwise. The feds tried to stop my group but here I am."

Daisy's mouth hung open as she moved closer and whispered, "What did you do?"

"You really want to know?"

"Yes, I won't tell anyone."

"All right, come over here." Adder led her over to the back of his van and darted his head as if inspecting for eavesdroppers. Adder leaned closer to Daisy.

"I was so tired of the platitudes and the phonies. We drummed in circles, got arrested for stopping traffic on the Golden Gate Bridge, and harassed Army recruiting centers and draft boards. But the war went on. And let me tell you, Big Oil was behind it all. Who benefits the most from war? The oil companies. They are the lifeblood of every instrument of death on the planet. War is good for slaves to the almighty dollar. The more death and destruction, the more their coffers are filled."

Daisy nodded in agreement. She winced every time Adder mentioned "Big Oil."

This was too easy.

"I'll never forget the spirit at Woodstock."

"Oh my God," Daisy interrupted. "You were at Woodstock?"

"Oh yeah, it was a time. We were all so free. In my mind, we would break down every government, right every wrong, and stop every injustice by spreading that spirit as far as we could."

"But it didn't turn out that way?"

"No. There were too many phonies who just wanted to get high. There's a time and place for that. But you have to stand for something. If there is no fight then what's the point? Too many times we talked, felt good, maybe made noise at a protest, and then went home, got stoned, and drowned our sorrows again. That's it and nothing's changed. *Planet Rescue*'s heart is in the right place but they're not willing to go the extra mile."

Daisy nodded after every word. "So what did you do?"

"Sure you want to find out?"

"Yeah. Tell me, please."

"Ok, listen. I got in with a group of radicals that realized if the fight was not taken to the government and Big Oil then nothing would ever change. We planted a few bombs in some refineries that caused massive damage. The problem was the oil executives got together and suppressed everything. It never made the news. They cleaned it up, pretending it never happened. If it had made it to the press that would have sparked a real revolution."

"Really?"

"Yeah, we did that. And much more."

Daisy's mouth gaped. Adder inspected the immediate area again then focused on her eyes and said, "I sense a real connection with you. It's biological or electric or something. For the first time in years I have met someone that actually cares about our planet."

"I do! This is who I am. And I feel it too. It's like destiny or something."

"Do you want to get in my van where we can talk more? I'll tell you everything."

Daisy's smile widened and her eyes softened. "I want you to show me everything," she replied, opening the van door.

I'm old enough to be her father, Adder thought. *Damn, this is too easy.*

Adder pushed down the shame brimming to the surface as he followed Daisy into his disgusting van. At least the pain would be numbed by something other than alcohol for a change.

CHAPTER 18

THE ENERGY IN THE RICHMOND, VA hotel banquet room was not quite peppy, but admirable. Peter Baylor was finishing his first policy speech as a candidate for senate. There were maybe a hundred people in the room, many with green and blue signs reading, "Baylor for Senate—A New Virginia for a Modern World." Baylor had little experience with delivering campaign speeches but had witnessed his mentor, Senator Boyd Radford, give thousands of them, many of which Peter wrote.

"One of the last things my good friend Boyd said, I'll never forget this, is, 'Peter, you can never stop fighting for what you stand for no matter what the cost,'" he said to an emotional crowd. "At that moment I never considered running for anything. I've always been a behind-the-scenes kind of guy. And working for Boyd was my lifelong ambition. We were doing important things and helping real people. I always said this was as good as it gets.

"And then tragedy occurred." Peter paused for effect. The crowd grew silent and hung their heads. Women put their hands over their mouths.

"Now I don't mean to bring this up to pull on heartstrings but I also can't ignore what was one of the most influential moments of my life. Everything came crashing down in an instant. I lost my boss, my mentor, and my best friend. And I had colleagues that said, 'Peter, no one would hold it against you if you quit fighting and live the quiet

life. You've done the best you can, but this tragedy is just
impossible to overcome.'"

"But they were wrong. I mourn my friend and grieve
for his loss but one thought kept ringing in my head: our
work is not done. We must continue to fight for the voice-
less, lift the unfortunate, and make America a shining
example of equality for the rest of the world."

The crowd applauded. Peter smiled, feeding off the
energy. Leaving his podium he held the microphone in
one hand and motioned to the crowd with the other as he
spoke.

"Now, I'm just a simple Virginia boy who grew up near
a farm. My parents always instilled in me strong values.
They said the key to life is helping other people even if that
means taking on the entire system. And I know our country
has made mistakes in the past. I need not get into the many
injustices we've inflicted on people of color, women, gays,
and our friends who come from another country looking
for a better life. And you know I'm committed to leveling
the playing field so every person has the right to healthcare,
education, and decent wages. But there's another issue that
has taken center stage that we need to handle right now.

"The oil in the Gulf of Mexico is still leaking at an
alarming rate. Our great President Lloyd Wilson is
working night and day on this issue. I can see the anguish
in his eyes when he talks about the leak. This catastrophe
is weighing on him as it is on me. And we cannot ever
stop pursuing those responsible for this heinous attack.
Yet, there is a level of misunderstanding between us that
must be ironed out through discussion and compromise.
There's no doubt about that. And while the right blames
religion for these attacks, progressives like you and me
know better. In times of a great loss, we must seek greater

understanding and forge a new path toward acceptance and celebration of our differences."

The crowd was eating out of his hand. Shouts of insults against the right combined with chants of "equality."

"That is not to say there are no bad people in this world. But, it is much more complicated than it seems. It is our duty to examine every underlying issue because we hold ourselves to a higher standard. And the fact of the matter is that oil derricks were targeted because oil companies have made us dependent on their product. They attack and belittle clean energy to increase profit margins. The system is rigged against the little guy who just wants to do their part to help the environment. But that ends today!"

The room beheld its biggest applause of the night. Some jumped up and down while others waved campaign signs. One couple even danced, pushing their arms up and down in the air as they moved about the room.

Peter motioned for the crowd to settle and continued, "Now at the risk of sounding cliché I want to quote a personal hero of mine, John Lennon. He said 'you may say I'm a dreamer but I'm not the only one' and that's one hundred percent true. I'm a dreamer. I dream big. And that's why if you put me into office I've got an ambitious environmental agenda that will scare those big oil companies right out of their $500 shoes!"

More applause exploded throughout the room.

"I will not rest until I push through a bill that bans the use of fracking!"

An even bigger applause erupted.

"And we will put a stop to deep sea oil exploration. They can't be attacked and inflict massive amounts of damage to our oceans and ecosystem if they are banished from our oceans. I will shake up the status quo and ban drilling in ANWR. I will push for a major carbon tax that will siphon revenues to clean, renewable energy like wind, solar, and hydroelectric. But we will not stop there! I am declaring war on the coal industry. This antiquated form of energy is already on the way out so let us hasten its demise. You and I will save this planet. The waters will stop rising, the air will be easier to breathe, and our children will have a clean and safe planet. Our generation will save planet Earth!"

The crowd whipped into a frenzy. For effect, Peter took the time to point and wave at no one in particular. After the crowd calmed, he continued, "But I'm not finished yet. People like you are the only reason these much needed reforms are possible. You are on the front lines to save this planet. That's why I will push for a huge tax break for owners of electric cars. We need to reward people like you and incentivize others to get in line with our pro-Earth agenda. I will also push automobile companies into making clean, electric vehicles and get rid of gas guzzlers that are making the hole in the ozone layer even bigger.

"Hey, like I said, I'm a dreamer. But with people like you at my side I know we can make these ambitious plans come to fruition. Our existence is at stake. Send me to Washington to reshape America into our own image! Thank you and goodnight!"

Peter Baylor roamed the stage for a few moments while the speakers blasted John Lennon's "Imagine." He shook hands, waved, and pointed at dozens of people before heading off the stage where a man in a dark gray suit waited. Peter acknowledged him with a head nod.

"Right this way, sir," he said to Peter. "They're waiting backstage."

Peter adjusted his tie and took a deep breath. The man led him to an adjoining lounge where seven people sat on plush couches. Each held a glass of wine or liquor. As he entered they set down their drinks to give Peter a standing ovation. Peter smiled and took a mock bow.

"Thank you," he said. "That crowd lifted me up. Our campaign is capturing real momentum."

Wasting no time, a burly man with a long, well kept beard stood and took command of the room, "Listen, Peter we're happy with that speech but we've got a few concerns."

Peter shook his head up and down; hoping the sweat forming on his brow was unnoticeable. "Yes. Let me put you at ease," he replied.

"First, what are your thoughts on 'Planet Rescue' and their protests across the country? Is this something you're looking to align with or not?"

"That's a great question and I'm glad you mentioned that. Their heart is in the right place and a lot of our grass-roots fundraising will use that same spirit. Our political base is eating that up. So—"

"If I may," the burly man interrupted. "Things might get a little out of control with 'Planet Rescue.'"

"Oh?"

"We would caution you to keep any endorsements of their activities to small, tight-knit fundraisers and closed-door sessions with no press in attendance."

Peter considered lashing out at the abrupt command before remembering who he was talking with. "Yes," he said. "I understand."

"Good," the man replied. "Second, where are you with Madison Gladstone's endorsement?"

Peter cleared his throat and shuffled. "Well, she's a tough nut to crack. I've spoken with her and I'm confident she will come around."

The burly man looked down his hook nose at Peter. "Peter, let me be blunt. There is a groundswell for her to be the nominee. And we're just getting started in this campaign. She could come in a week before the primary filing date and take this thing. If you don't get her on board, then that will make us very nervous."

Peter swallowed and said nothing. He wanted to curse Madison for her insolence.

"We have other plans for her but our sources tell us she's a real wildcard," the man continued. "She's become increasingly unpredictable since Boyd Radford screwed us and took the easy way out."

"Ok, I understand," Peter said.

"Do you?" The man asked, irritated. "The stakes are too high. We won't let our plans result in failure."

The rest of the people in the room all nodded with sullen looks.

"I get it, I do," Peter said. "She will come around. I'll handle her."

"We're glad to hear that, Peter. See that you do."

CHAPTER 19

ONE OF THE FEW TIMES MADISON'S mind felt clear was during her daily jog. She never considered herself a fitness nut but the distraction from her hectic life was always welcome. The resulting exhaustion drained tension and worry. Yet, today's run was spoiled after Madison caught Special Agent Walter Robinson watching her jog toward her office building with his sunglasses pulled down and nodding. "Oh, for God's sake," Madison said under her breath.

Walter turned as she approached; unaware he had been totally busted. Madison slowed to a walk. Catching her breath, she greeted him and said, "So what do you have for me today, Walt?" He failed to notice her eyes rolling.

Walter cleared his throat. "Well, there are some new developments. Might we talk inside?"

Madison took a deep breath. "Yes, of course. Let me get a quick shower at the Capitol gym and I'll meet you in my office."

Later the two sat in opposing chairs in front of her desk. Walter fidgeted like a schoolboy sent to the principal's office. The top button over his tie laid unbuttoned and his suit appeared to have been slept in the night prior. The dark circles under his eyes accentuated his unshaven face as he tapped his fingers nervously.

"What's going on?" Madison asked. "Let's get on with this."

"Yes, yes I'm sorry," Walter replied shakily. "Remember how I told you I am being pressured to drop this case?

Well, someone is turning up the heat. I get the feeling some higher up FBI officials are involved."

"Where is this originating from?"

"That's the thing. I'm not sure. But now I'm even getting casual comments to drop it from agents that aren't involved with this investigation. I find it hard to believe this is uncoordinated. And my supervisors have flat-out ordered me to wrap it up."

"So why don't you?" Madison was at a loss for words. For a moment, she wondered if it would be best for everyone if this case came to a close. Boyd's death involved many disturbing details for sure, but whose suicide did not?

Sensing Madison's frustration, Walter nodded and stared at the ground. Sheepishly, he replied, "Because something is still nagging me. I've hit a dead end. But perhaps it's because someone is working against everything I do. It's a delicate situation, no doubt."

Madison sighed, tapping her fingers in the same fidgety motion as Walter. "Ok, what can we do to resolve this situation?"

Walter's hopeful eyes met Madison's. The gut feeling pulling inside was enough to keep going. This case should have been open and shut but something lingered—something nefarious. Walter understood it would fester unless a solution came forth.

"Maybe there is something you can help with. You know Jeanne, Boyd's wife, right? I spoke with her recently."

Madison thought of seeing Jeanne at Boyd's funeral. The world seemed to crash with her despair. They had spent many nights at dinner or some function with their husbands. They would discuss dresses, family, commitment, and many other topics. But never politics. Jeanne understood the political world better than anyone. Politics made her husband happy, and that was a great sense of joy for Jeanne. That did not mean politics had a warm place in her heart though. Jeanne found beauty in almost everything. That was her special gift. When you search for elegance and mirth in everyday life, politics will not appear on your radar. Madison had never seen love drain from Jeanne's face as it did during Boyd's funeral. It shook Madison to the core.

"She's a good woman," Madison said under her breath. "I can't imagine the pain Jeanne is feeling right now. Did she give you anything useful?"

"Not much. But maybe I was not asking the right questions. Boyd's suicide had something to do with you, but I'm grasping at straws right now. Would you chat with Jeanne? Maybe you will have better luck. I really need more information about the email that refers to protecting you. That's the only lead I have, if you can even call it that."

Madison sighed and sat back. Jeanne was a sweetheart, the consummate politician's wife. Behind closed doors she was as supportive of Boyd as in public. The sacrifices associated with politics were readily accepted. Jeanne loved her husband even though she missed him during eighty-plus-hour weeks or on some major campaign tour. But she never once chastised him. Jeanne understood the importance of his work to the people of Virginia.

Madison also possessed a touch of guilt. She had checked in on Jeanne a few times since Boyd's death but not enough in her estimation. Madison sometimes blamed herself for his suicide although the reasons why were unclear. She would sacrifice anything to get answers. Jeanne deserved that. The American people deserved that.

"Ok, I'll talk with her," Madison said.

Walter smiled.

The next day, Madison drove out to the Radfords' home in Great Falls, VA. The gated mansion sat in one of the most posh neighborhoods in the state. Residents included legislators, ambassadors, and other dignitaries. The Secretary of State had a home close to the Radfords'. The Austrian embassy kept a house two doors down for whenever government officials visited Washington.

Madison remembered the access code to the gate. Jeanne made it clear that Madison had free range to come and go as she pleased. Madison drove close to the front door of the four-story mega-house, exited, took a deep breath, and rang the doorbell. A full two minutes passed before a scurrying from behind the door preceded a bleary-eyed Jeanne answering.

Jeanne's eyes may have been red from crying, but her natural beauty did not wane. Jeanne was tall, refined, and unafraid to show graying hair that suited her better than most. She looked the part of a strong wife to a powerful political leader. Her soft eyes widened at the sight of Madison.

"Maddy!" Jeanne almost cried. "It's so good to see you, please come in."

Madison entered and embraced Jeanne with a strong hug. "Hi, Jeanne, I'm so sorry I haven't come around more."

"Now stop that. You're doing big important things and I know Boyd…" She released Madison, covering her face with a wispy hand. She motioned for Madison to enter. Speaking softly, Jeanne continued, "…he would have wanted you to keep fighting the good fight. I'm sorry. I can't seem to get it together today!"

Madison's heart broke all over again as it had during Boyd's funeral. Madison had a special relationship with her mentor but Jeanne shared her life with the senator. If the hole in Madison's heart was massive, how big was Jeanne's? "You have nothing to be sorry about. I can come back another time."

Jeanne sniffed and cleared her throat. "Nonsense. Please come in, I need a friend."

Madison smiled and followed Jeanne to an adjacent sitting room. The Radford home was always neat and orderly. Each room was a museum to hundreds of great accomplishments and experiences. Photos littered the walls of the couple meeting a dignitary or enjoying an exotic trip. The picture with Elvis Presley was Madison's favorite. Although, the snapshot of Boyd in the Oval Office with Ronald Reagan was a close second.

"Would you like tea?" Jeanne asked.

"Oh, no thanks. Your company will be more than enough."

Jeanne smiled, mouthing "thank you" while wiping tears from her eyes. They sat on a plush brown leather sofa that was in such great condition it looked like it had never been used. The room was as quiet as a library aside from the ticking from the grandfather clock in the corner. The mantle over the marble fireplace had once held pictures of great political accomplishments; Boyd on the senate floor or at a bill signing. Jeanne replaced all of those with pictures of the two of them, some going as far back as their youth. They met during college summer vacation over forty years ago. Although they were both from the same small town, they had never met. A mutual friend introduced them at a drive-in restaurant and that was all it took. They were married a few months later.

Madison and Jeanne exchange pleasantries, discussing topics ranging from weather to reality television. In a few moments the pair seemed like old friends catching up without a care in the world. But on the inside Madison was filled with dread. "Jeanne," Madison started, "I hate to bring this up and if this causes any pain, please stop me and we can forget it, but..."

"You want to talk about Boyd?" Jeanne interrupted.

Madison smiled with sad eyes. "I want to be honest. An FBI agent is investigating Boyd's death."

Jeanne nodded. "Oh yes, that nice Walt fellow?"

"Yes, Walter Robinson."

"He was very respectful when we chatted."

Madison's smile grew. "I'm glad to hear that, he's a good man." Madison remembered wanting to punch Walter the first time they spoke. The sense of duty and devotion he showed to Boyd made her regret her initial anger.

"I'm sorry they've dragged you into this," Jeanne said, reaching for a tissue from her pocket. "I have gone over every minute from the last month prior to Boyd's death in my head, trying to find a reason for... you know. But... it's my fault. How did I not see this coming?"

Madison opened her mouth to protest but Jeanne waved, "Now stop. I know what you're going to say. But there is no way anyone in my position could not blame themselves. That's a natural reaction to tragedy. Plus it's true. I'm his wife for God's sake! If I did not sense his pain then who could have?"

Madison fought back tears. She focused on the floor for a moment, trying to find words. "I'm so sorry, Jeanne. I can't imagine the pain you must be going through."

"Yes, you can. You loved Boyd. Not in the same way as I did, but he thought of you as a daughter. And after everything that happened between you and your father, you saw him as more than a mentor. You loved him like family, didn't you?"

Madison nodded. The tears swelled in her eyes. She quickly thought of the driest piece of legislation she ever voted for. It worked. Thinking about the silliness of voting to rename an Alaskan Post Office after Susan B. Anthony in a town of twenty-three tricked her mind into focusing on anything but grief. Did Congress not have better things to do?

"Did Walter tell you about the email?"

Jeanne nodded. "Walter told me how an unaddressed email said something to the effect of him trying to protect you."

"Exactly."

"And I take it you have no idea what that concerned?"

"It's been killing me. I haven't a clue. And believe me, there's enough guilt to go around. If I led him to… what happened… I'll never forgive myself."

"I've thought a lot about this too," Jeanne said with a sigh. "Whenever Boyd spoke of you it was with glowing admiration. He always said you were doing great things. And I imagine Boyd wanted to protect you in many ways.

"What I do know is he worked himself too hard. There would be weeks where he would get a big win in a campaign or on the Hill and was so happy, so fun to be around. Then other times he'd shut down over some political crisis. But he always managed to survive. The most upset I ever saw him occurred after the blowup with your father. But, I'm sorry; I don't mean to bring up old wounds."

"No, please, this might be important. Go on."

Jeanne blotted her eyes with the tissue. "Well, all right. It happened right in this very room. Boyd was here with your dad and Boyd's chief of staff, Peter Baylor."

"Peter, really?" Madison's sadness turned to anger. There was a good reason she disliked Peter so much. He always found himself in precarious situations. How had Boyd put up with him for so long?

"Yes, Peter was there. And he sided with your dad."

"Are you kidding me? That little snake!" Wrong again, Peter.

"I never liked him." Jeanne shook her head. "Whenever I asked Boyd why he kept that conniving little twerp in his circle, he just said you needed people like that to get things done in DC. Boyd didn't like the shady part of politics but that's how the game is played."

"So why did he cut off ties with my dad but not Peter?"

"Peter wasn't as forceful. He said, 'you realize, he's got a point' and things like that. Your dad and Boyd were about to brawl though. They didn't speak after that."

Madison was taken aback. "I never heard the full story, just fragments really. What were they actually fighting about?"

"I think it had something to do with your dad's political organization. But it was an enormous deal. I think the fight concerned that as much as anything else. I never pried into Boyd's political affairs. Although, now I wish I had. Maybe I could have helped his suffering."

"My heart is just so broken for your, Jeanne." She imagined this was how Walter's conversation with Jeanne went. How much can you accost a grieving widow about her deceased husband?

"I'm sorry, Madison. I don't know if that's helpful at all."

Everyone in politics works with some shady individuals. Some are more disreputable than others. Madison noted that a blowup of this magnitude must have been the result of something truly unscrupulous. Bitter feuds happen all the time in public for the benefit of the political game. But behind closed doors those feuds are nothing more than show for the cameras. "Perhaps Boyd hid his anguish better than most. I'll always regret not being able to help."

"Me too." Jeanne coughed and stroked her chest just below her neck.

Madison rose. "I should be going."

"I understand."

"I'll come back soon. I mean that."

"You're doing important things, my dear. It's okay, really."

Madison did not have the words. She hugged Jeanne and walked to the door. This house had once been filled with such happiness. Now, it was a memorial to a fallen American hero. Before leaving, Madison turned to Jeanne and asked, "Are you sure you don't remember any more details about what Boyd and my dad were working on?"

Jeanne looked to the ceiling in thought and crossed her arms. "Well now that you mention it, it's possible it involved a business deal. They often spoke of purchasing or starting a business. Maybe it wasn't political at all. He shied away from discussing details, and I never asked, but all I remember is it supposedly would change everything. That's what he said anyway. He was tense but excited before their relationship fell apart. That must sound bizarre, but he only discussed it a few times with me."

"So it had nothing to do with dad's political organization?"

"No, it did, I think. But it involved some business deal as well. I'm sorry, Maddy, that's not at all helpful."

"And that's all you remember?"

Jeanne shrugged her shoulders. "My memory is not what it used to be. The details are hazy."

Madison hugged Jeanne again. "Thanks for your time. It means a lot. And it's awful of me quizzing you like this. I just..."

"I know," Jeanne interrupted. "I miss him too. And I want answers as much as you do."

Madison lamented hitting another dead end as she headed toward her car. Jeanne waited in the doorway, watching.

Before Madison could leave the house, Jeanne shouted, "I just remembered something!"

"Oh?"

"There were two other partners in that deal. Senator Tom Mullen and some congresswoman. Umm... Fran *something*, Fran Norris!"

CHAPTER 20

"HE WILL BE HERE, YOU'LL SEE," the man with the code name Adder said to Daisy. He pushed her golden hair back over her left ear. She wore a huge smile and stroked his chest with a light touch. They passionately kissed.

No one in the raucous crowd even seemed to notice the couple. They positioned themselves in the back of what amounted to be around a hundred heated protesters. Many held signs with various environmental messages and anti-capitalist slurs. The *Planet Rescue* leader who spoke with the crowd the other day stood atop the hood of a car and screamed platitudes and led chants. Even with his megaphone it proved difficult to hear over the loud and boisterous crowd.

The scene was total hysteria. Some peaceful protesters played drums in a circle near the back. Most were whipped up on various drugs and wore the eyes of killers. They bounced up and down in front of a gated fracking site a mile from their camp in the hills of Pennsylvania. Guards lined the inside of the ominous fence and police were en route. The media had the cameras rolling from every angle.

In the previous days, Adder had sunk his teeth into many of these "useful idiots," as he referred to them. It was almost as easy as brainwashing Daisy. Adder realized the magnitude of these actions would hit him later when he would inevitably fall into a drunken haze of guilt. But in the moment he would maintain absolute professionalism. He had a job to do and his training would not let him focus on anything but the mission. Soon it would be all over. There were always potential curveballs thrown at the last minute, but with every passing second the chances of something going wrong became less likely.

Adder hugged Daisy and slipped the package under her coat in the back of her pants. Adder made the delivery with such a fluid motion that even a trained eye would have had trouble reading the situation.

"You have yours too, right?" Daisy whispered.

"That's the plan," he replied as he slid back from his hug and gently embraced her face with the palm of his hand.

Daisy shook nervously. Tagging along for these protests was supposed to be about having fun and gaining life experience during summer vacation. Never in her darkest dreams did she imagine she would commit such a deed. But this was love. And the dying planet could not wait for a savior any longer.

Adder sensed her hesitancy. "Listen, you can do this," he reassured her. "I can read people, it's a gift. You have more strength than I've ever seen. This is the start of the revolution to save the planet."

Daisy continued to shake. "Look, I want to be a part of this, I do. It's just that…"

Oh boy, thought Adder. *Here we go.*

"…I don't want to go to prison. I can't save the planet from there."

"That won't happen. You'll see. We'll slip away into the crowd and meet back at my van. I have a place we can hideout for a few days until things settle down. From there, we'll travel with a few like-minded groups from here to California. It's the perfect plan and we'll be long gone before everything settles. That's when we'll decide our next move. We will see things like this happening everywhere.

The revolution will be in full swing and it will be more than the authorities can handle; they will forget all about today's victory. It will be glorious!"

Daisy still appeared unsure. She stared at the ground with a frown as tears came rolling down.

"Listen, there's one more thing I need to tell you but I'm scared," Adder said with as much false sincerity as he could muster.

"What?" Daisy looked up at him with adoring eyes once again.

"I love you."

Daisy lit up. That youthful smile returned.

"We just met and truthfully, I've never been in love before, but you make me feel alive. Together, we will do something I've never been able to accomplish. I realize now I needed my soulmate to help reach this level. I love you so much."

Daisy threw her arms around his neck. He lifted her off the ground and twirled her in the air. She kissed him repeatedly.

"I love you too, Jonas. This is the best day of my life."

"Mine too."

"Ok, can we go over it one more time?"

Got her.

"Sure. Circle around to the left. Join in the crowd, shouting and chanting. Make your way to the front. When the crowd storms the gates make sure you're close to the front. When the target appears, you'll know what to do. You'll go first because you've got a better angle, plus if anything goes wrong, I can finish the job."

Determination flooded Daisy's face. "Ok, I'll do it. Gosh, Jonas, this is so exciting. I love you so much."

"I love you too. Now remember, you won't see me in the crowd but I will be there. I blend in well. Don't look for me either or you will give everything away. I'm counting on you."

"Ok, let's do it."

Adder gave Daisy one more kiss and watched as she slunk into the crowd, disappearing into the melee.

The speaker pushed the protesters to the verge of a riot. They swayed back and forth like waves in the ocean. Fists and protest signs filled the air.

"And we will not stop until fracking is shut down for good!" The lead protester yelled into his megaphone. "Are you with me, brothers and sisters?"

"*Yeah*!" They cried in loud unison.

"Let's do this! Storm the gates!"

In an instant, the crowd complied. The sturdy fifteen-feet-high fence boasted sharp barbed wire. But that did not stop the guards on the other side from feeling anxious. Many drew their nightsticks. The media flooded toward the gates as well, recording everything. The protesters tried scaling the fence with little luck. Instead, they settled for shaking the gate back and forth. The fence was solid, and the attempt was more for dramatic purposes anyway.

After a few minutes, a caravan of three black SUVs came rolling toward the gate from behind the fence. The vehicles pulled in front of the protesters and a single figure emerged from the back of the middle vehicle. The short, balding man wore glasses and a fine suit. He adjusted his tie and walked nervously toward the gate. The guards made way as he paused a few feet away from the snarling protesters.

The man waved in the air to settle the crowd. They failed to oblige, becoming more disorderly by the minute.

Agitated but determined, the man received a megaphone from a nearby guard.

After fumbling with the buttons, he had the guard show him how to use the loud speaker before waving him away. Speaking into the device, he looked toward the cameras and said, "Hello? Hello? Can you hear me?"

The crowd screamed louder with primal rage.

"Please let me speak. I understand your anger, care about your concerns, and am committed to making things right."

The crowd quieted. Some still jumped on and off the fence but many stopped to listen.

"You and I both share the same concern for the environment," he said.

The crowd booed and shook their fists.

"We are working with the Environmental Protection Agency on a study to show the world how fracking does not affect drinking water. What we are doing is safe and has a minor impact on the environment."

The boos grew louder. The protesters focused so much on the man they did not notice the busloads of police officers in riot gear arrive and deploy close to where Adder and Daisy had stood a few moments ago.

"I am here to ask you to please disperse," the man continued. "I will speak to a delegation of your choosing after you leave. This is an ongoing conversation we are happy to make and I—"

BANG! BANG! BANG!

Three shots exploded from Daisy's gun. The man imploring the crowd to leave dropped his megaphone. His perfectly starched white shirt slowly turned red as he dropped to his knees and slumped to the ground. Guards surrounded and pulled him into one of the black SUVs which quickly sped away.

Daisy dropped her gun and turned toward the crowd. Protesters ran in every direction. The media pushed forward, trying to get a shot of the attack. The police moved in just as quick. They took down everyone they could get their hands on. Daisy scanned the crowd and tried to find Jonas. He was supposed to have fired too but was nowhere to be seen. The police formed a perimeter around the crowd. No one would escape. Daisy cried hysterically after being tackled and handcuffed.

Later, Adder would hear about the incident on the radio. He was miles away before the first shots were fired. An hour later he confirmed his mission was a complete success when it was announced that Cody Finnan, the CEO of the largest fracking company in the world, died after suffering three gunshot wounds while trying to calm down a bloodthirsty *Planet Rescue* crowd.

The price of a barrel of oil would hit a record high by the time the stock market closed the next day.

CHAPTER 21

IT WAS A PERFECT NIGHT FOR a concert. The moon was full, the night air cool, and Bailee had her best voice. After two hours of music in front of a wild crowd of thousands, each madly screaming, Bailee was spent. She pranced off the stage with a huge smile, ready for more hassle waiting backstage. The next few minutes were spent displaying the public persona she carefully crafted over the years. Bailee thought of the heartache and sacrifice she had to endure. But it was worth it to become the top female vocalist in the world. The pop star boasted millions of fans, top-charting hits, and a business empire that spanned three continents.

But as everything does, it came with a cost. Bailee's entourage already badgered her with questions and reminders about this or that. Bailee loathed them for their falsities. These leeches who suckled at her success would dispense the minute she lost relevance, which she admitted would come someday. That was the inevitability of stardom. No one stayed on top forever. But a short foray was better than perpetual obscurity. And that is why she put up with the facade. Bailee determined to power through and stay relevant for as long as possible. She already had all but ended her marriage over questionable decisions, but her public persona would not suffer. She and Kronik would divorce somewhere down the road when it was helpful for both of their careers. But for now they would keep up the lies for the sake of the people.

Bailee made her way to the dressing room as the entourage increased in size. She entered to find at least two dozen people milling around on cellphones, working with backup dancers, while others snorted lines of coke and slammed tequila shots. Bailee sat in front of her makeup mirror and closed her eyes as the leeches continued to bicker.

We need to talk about your wardrobe for tomorrow's concert.

Your charity benefit for next month has to be rescheduled.

The samples for your Fall collection are coming in from Vietnam tomorrow morning.

Your music label wants to do the photoshoot for your next album in Milan.

Yadda. Yadda. Yadda.

It was all just noise. Bailee did her best to tune them out.

"Bailee." One of her assistants got her attention by handing the star a cellphone. "It's *him*."

Bailee snatched the phone, held it to her ear, and said, "Hold on" as she covered the speaker with her hand. She stood and waved while snapping. "Okay, everyone, give me the room, please?"

Most of the onlookers looked stunned, although a few of the drunkards barely registered any reaction. But they understood their place as they dutifully headed toward the door without delay. After a minute, she had relative quiet. Bailee took a deep breath and calmed her nerves. She snickered to herself after realizing she performed with no fear in front of 10,000 people or more but the man on the other end of the line gave her butterflies.

Bailee lifted the phone to her ear and said, "I'm so sorry about that, I wanted privacy."

"That's a rare commodity for both of us," the voice on the other end snorted. "I'm hiding in my private bathroom right now. This is the only place I can go without a watchful eye."

"It's good to hear from you, Mr. President," Bailee responded.

President Wilson sighed, "Call me, Lloyd."

"You have a strong name, but you've got the best title in the world. Might as well use it."

"Hmm. So, how are you? Did the concert go well?"

"It was fine. I don't even know what city I'm in right now though."

"Boulder, Colorado."

Bailee smiled. "You follow my tour?"

"When I get a chance. Tell no one though, you're my dirty little secret."

Bailee blushed. "Oh, Lloyd... I assume this isn't a social call though, is it?"

"It is and it isn't. I wanted to thank you for all the work you have been doing to support my efforts to stop this oil leak. It's been a real bear."

"I know, and this crisis breaks my heart. I can't imagine what you're going through."

"Well, that comes with the territory of being president."

"I get it." Bailee truly was upset with the situation. With all her power and money she could not stop the greatest environmental disaster of the time. The President of the United States did not seem to have that power either. There is nothing more frustrating to public figures with enormous ego than facing situations beyond their control.

"Also, I wanted to ask you another favor," the president continued. "Something I hope you'll keep between us, okay?"

"You know I'll do anything for you."

Now it was the president's turn to blush. Bailee sensed it over the phone.

President Wilson cleared his throat and said, "I need you to stop supporting *Planet Rescue*, okay?"

Bailee was taken aback. Not only had she done commercials and fundraisers for the organization but she mentioned their website at every concert. She had sung their praises since they were spotlighted by Reginald Goldsmith. "Why? They are the hottest ticket right now and are getting tons of press. This isn't about that Pennsylvania thing is it? Wasn't that an isolated incident?"

"For the time being. But the violence will escalate. There's a war on oil and it will only get worse. People are pissed but the economy must roll on. Next year, I'm up for reelection and this is the last thing I need. I have to distance myself from *Planet Rescue* but I can't denounce them, I'd get killed in the polls with my base. I've talked with friends running the news networks and they've agreed to tone the coverage down."

"That was nice of them."

"Hey, that's the media. They're like dogs. You give them a treat and a belly rub now and then and they'll show nothing but loyalty."

Baillee laughed.

"What?" The president asked.

"I had a mental image of you giving Reginald Goldsmith a belly rub."

Now the president laughed. Bailee noted that reaction was probably never heard in public. Lloyd's real laugh was adorable. His voice squeaked as he breathed in and out like a mongoose. Bailee loved it.

"So what else can I do?" Bailee asked after the president's chuckles subsided.

"Maybe we could set up a few more PSAs and a fundraiser for my reelection bid? We can tie it to the cleanup."

"I'd be happy to do that, you know that."

"Ok, my people will call your people, so to speak."

"Sounds good."

"Listen, Bailee, I appreciate this. Hopefully, we can get together again soon."

"I'd love that."

The president hesitated then softly said, "Me too."

They both blushed—one more time.

CHAPTER 22

"DO YOU HAVE AN APPOINTMENT?" THE receptionist asked Madison as she entered the office of California Senator Tom Mullen.

Madison's lips thinned. "Yes."

"Your name?"

Madison felt like she was at the dentist. She guessed this was just how some Senate offices worked. Or maybe the lack of decorum was based on the fact that Capitol Hill was really run by twenty-somethings not yet burned out in politics. Kids fresh from college wrote the legislation that left these buildings. That's a fact most Americans would abhor if they paid any attention.

"I'm Representative Madison Gladstone," she said to the twenty-something receptionist.

"Oh yes, go on in, the senator is waiting for you."

Madison rolled her eyes as she passed through the big oak door. Mullen's office was large but still conservative, as far as offices of powerful people went. The power players in DC kept illusions of honesty and humility. The extravagance of decor was normally confined to the more secretive lairs of power.

"Madison, it's a pleasure, please sit." Senator Mullen stood from behind his desk and motioned for her to take a seat in a row of leather chairs toward the back of his office. He followed and took an opposing seat.

Mullen was a staple on Capitol Hill. He had held office for the State of California since before Madison was born.

The senator idolized Ted Kennedy and it showed in his policies and campaign positions. On occasion, he would even throw out a slight Boston accent in speeches even though he was from Sacramento. The media never called him on it but right-wing bloggers always had a field day.

Tom's puffed white hair was curly and his neck drooped like a turkey, but his face showed little sign of wear for a man his age. The fortune spent on Botox must have been sizeable. But after decades in public service, he could afford such luxuries. Heck, he probably got them for free. His eyes were worse than *Mr. Magoo* but he only wore glasses in private to avoid the appearance of old age. Tom's image was that of a fighter and go-getter who pulled out all the stops. It was a carefully crafted persona shaped by years of public relations professionals and campaign consultants.

But Mullen forged his own legacy and had some of the best political instincts in the country. Many said, if he had not been from California and had more centrist appeal he could have been president. He flirted with that idea, as everyone on Capitol Hill does at one point or another, but put that dream to rest after a few rumors involving young, blonde senate aides made it into a certain news magazine. The reporter's career never recovered but the court of public opinion banished Mullen to his nothing higher than senatorial duties until his death.

Mullen wore his trademark smile as he crossed his legs and eyed Madison up and down as she took her seat. Madison was used to being ogled by DC's dirty old men, but that did not mean she approved.

Madison was unsure how to start this conversation but luckily Mullen was in a forceful mood. "So, I understand your committee is getting close to a decision on the Keystone Pipeline." That was not a question.

"Yes, Senator, should be a few more weeks."

"Let me be frank, that will eat us up if it comes to a vote. We can't be seen supporting more oil and gas exploration and transportation while the Gulf is filled up with bubbly stuff. Our base will kill us if the Republicans push this through. They only need two votes in committee."

Mullen eyed her down, dancing around the issue for as long as possible without asking her to vote his way. In a different time, Madison would play the game, but that would defeat the purpose of the visit.

"I have not yet decided which way to vote," she said point blank. "My constituents worry about the increase in gas prices. We are seeing the national average approach $4.00 and a lot of experts in the financial sector, including my husband I might add, believe $7.00 gas is in the cards before the end of the year. If that happens then *you* might even face a tough reelection."

They both laughed.

"Well, let me worry about that," Mullen said as he removed his glasses for effect. "All I'm saying is we need more time. If you can push to delay the final vote then I can line up a better strategy in the senate. I'd like to work with you on this one."

Madison hesitated then replied, "Ok, I can do that." She had to play ball to get what she really wanted out of this meeting. It was not an enormous request but that type of good will would go far in this city.

"Excellent!" Mullen said, standing to indicate the end of the meeting. Madison had used the Keystone Pipeline as a pretense for the sit-down but she needed information.

"Senator, if I may, I wanted to ask you about Boyd Radford."

Without missing a beat, Mullen said, "You have my deepest condolences. I know you two were close. He was a good man, and an even better friend."

Tom stood with arms crossed. The senator appeared ready for Madison's questions. But how could that be? Maybe the polished politician in him was prepared for anything. Or maybe not.

"Thank you," Madison said, showing visible emotion. "I do miss him very much. And there are still so many questions."

"We all want answers. Boyd was a remarkable leader. He *should* have been president if his stubbornness had not gotten in the way."

That was an odd thing to say, Madison noted.

For a moment, Madison noticed a look of a worry in Senator Mullen's eyes. He then walked back to his desk while averting his eyes.

"Oh?" Madison retorted. She stood and circled to the front of his desk as the senator shuffled papers. "Boyd considered a run at one point?"

Mullen coughed. "Oh no, not that I knew of."

"But you said his *stubbornness* got in the way of running."

"Well, you know, too stubborn to think about it. But he would have been good for the job. Boyd's centrism would have had broad appeal yet he was with us on *most* issues."

The pair awkwardly stared at each other for a moment.

"I spoke with his wife, Jeanne, the other day," Madison said, cutting the tension. She needed to probe for further kernels of truth.

"Oh? And how is she doing? I sent her a letter after Boyd's death and meant to call her soon."

"She's doing as well as expected under the circumstances. She's always been a fighter."

"That she is." Mullen smiled and nodded.

"Jeanne said you and Boyd were working on something big together at one point recently. Would you mind sharing some details? Maybe it's important."

Senator Mullen stopped shuffling his papers and sat. He clasped his fingers in a point and stared at Madison right in her eyes. "Well, nothing out of the ordinary, just politics as usual."

"Did it concern a specific piece of legislation or a business deal perhaps?"

Mullen cocked his head ever so slightly and replied, "Well, I have not thought about it since he passed. I will get back to you about that another time."

"Hmm, very well. You sure you don't—"

"Nope," Mullen interrupted. "I will contact you if I can remember anything."

Senator Mullen spotted something of obvious importance on his desk and turned his full attention to a paper. He picked it up and swung his chair away from Madison, who still stood like a schoolgirl in the principal's office. She had been dismissed.

Pompous ass, Madison thought to herself as she let herself out of Mullen's office. Something did not seem right about that meeting. But before Madison got her bearings, she opened the outer door into the hallway of the senate building and stood face to face with Rep. Fran Norris.

"Oh, Madison, it's so good to run into you!" Fran said.

"You too," Madison replied while gazing up and down the hallway. Not another soul was in sight. Not totally unusual, but odd.

"You really should have joined me at that Bailee concert, it was extraordinary!" Fran said with a smile. "I dreaded it but I rather enjoyed the show. She has some incredible vocals."

"That she does. Fran, it's good to see you but I need to go."

"There are always places to be around here, Madison. I wonder though, do you have twenty minutes? There is something I'd like to discuss with you."

Madison felt a strange mix of worry and intrigue. Jeanne mentioned that Fran had been involved with whatever Boyd had been working on with her father. After the strange meeting with Tom Mullen, Madison convinced herself something bizarre happened as a result of that deal. Maybe it related to Boyd's death. Although reluctant, she agreed to join Fran. She laid out her hand palm up, gesturing to lead the way.

Fran led her down the hallway to a set of stairs leading to the basement. Two floors down they reached a group of private offices not unlike where the national security briefing with the mysterious frumpy man was held. Fran marched to a door marked with just the number three and led her into a plush, windowless, but well-lit room. The office seemed modest aside from fine leather sofas lining the walls. A small conference table surrounded by eight chairs sat in front of a large wooden desk. An American flag rested behind the desk along with the New York state flag.

Fran sat on the nearest couch.

Madison followed her lead. "Where are we exactly?" she asked.

"This is an annex office for Senator Brahm." Chuck Brahm was the senior senator from New York and next in line to be majority leader. "We're good friends. He lets me use this space whenever I want."

"How nice of him. You seem to be cordial with a lot of Democrats, Fran. That is rare on the Hill these days." Madison had never spoken with Brahm aside from a few words at the White House Christmas party. Brahm's haughty demeanor made Madison's skin crawl. The senior senator never associated with people that could not give him what he wanted at that particular moment. Thus far, Madison had not fallen into that camp. That was fine by her.

"Well, like I've said before, politics is not as blood-thirsty behind these walls as most people believe."

"So what can I do for you?" Madison said, shorter than intended.

Fran smiled. "Tom Mullen is a friend of mine as well and he mentioned your meeting today. I must admit that I waited for you outside his office."

Madison crossed her arms and legs. "I figured. But why?"

"Your father, Tom, and I were working with Boyd on something. We wanted to keep it on the down low though."

Finally, she was getting somewhere. "What?"

"We discussed a primary challenge to President Wilson."

"Wait, what?" Madison failed to hide her shock. Many questions flew through her mind. Two Democratic sena-tors were working with a Republican congresswoman to mount a primary challenge against the sitting Democratic president? Madison accepted Fran's notion of odd political alliances behind closed doors but this seemed too much. Every Republican dreams of a Democrat challenging a

Democratic president just as Democrats love the same idea for a Republican president. But no elected official would work with someone in the opposite party to make it happen. Would they?

"There are some serious doubts in the ranks he can win another term," Fran said, sensing Madison's skepticism.

"Well, you're a Republican, that's an expected position."

"It's more than that, dear. The GOP's field of candidates is weak. For my own reasons, I can't get behind any of them. They're either creeps behind closed doors or they're too far away from what I consider must be done for this country. I'm more pro-environment than most Republicans will admit, and this whole oil crisis in the Gulf has me rethinking a lot of policies. And I fear Lloyd Wilson does not possess the political capital to take care of things. His administration is losing credibility by the day. We need to take drastic action to right the ship. And if that means I help get a Democrat elected then so be it."

"So you wanted Boyd to primary Wilson?"

"That was mentioned, yes."

"I don't understand. Did that have anything to do with his suicide?"

Fran hesitated for a split second and cleared her throat.

"No, I don't think so. I thought I should mention it since you are so troubled by his death. We never got into planning stages anyway. Challenging a sitting president in a primary is almost impossible. But these types of conversations are commonplace and they usually just end naturally."

Madison sighed. Her mind had raced toward conspiracy theories. Nothing about what she learned concerning the circumstances surrounding Boyd's death made sense. Maybe she had not been exposed to this side of politics in full detail.

For the first time, Madison wondered if this so-called plot surrounding Boyd's suicide was all in her head.

CHAPTER 23

PRESIDENT LLOYD WILSON STARED OUT THE window of the Oval Office with obvious concern following his daily briefing on the oil spill in the Gulf of Mexico. The latest scheme involved dumping millions of used golf balls into one of the holes. Wilson shook his head imagining all those golf balls floating to the ocean floor. Predictably, it was a complete failure.

The president was aware this job would be the most stressful thing he had ever done. That came with the territory. He campaigned for the opportunity to occupy this seat in the White House. Right now the words his predecessor told him on Inauguration Day reverberated: "Every day you will break but you can't ever let it show." Wilson thought himself strong but he sensed his presidency crashing. With every passing day he glimpsed at declining approval ratings, something he should never do, and it troubled him to no end.

Wilson experienced tight spots before and stressful dealings were more to come. There was no other choice than to move forward. He believed he could deal with anything. That's why the American people put their faith in him in the first place, he decided.

"All right then," he said standing and adjusting his tie. He buzzed his secretary, "Joyce, send in the Saudi Ambassador please."

"Yes, Mr. President."

Saudi Ambassador Abdulaziz was also a member of the royal family. He lived most of his adult life in the United States and was keenly aware of the cultural and political differences between the two countries. Really, he was perfect for the job. President Wilson liked Abdulaziz but this would be an uncomfortable discussion. That also went with the territory of being president.

"Welcome Ambassador, please take a seat," the president said with a smile as the Saudi entered the Oval Office from the concealed door.

The ambassador was dressed in a fine handmade suit. The cost must have been exorbinant. They shook hands as the ambassador made his way to one of the main couches. "Thank you, Mr. President, it's good to see you. I realize your time is valuable and I appreciate the meeting."

"Anything for our Saudi friends," the president replied as he sat on the opposite couch to the ambassador. "Now, what can I do for you?"

Abdulaziz was a smooth operator. He studied at Oxford and his English was impeccable. The ambassador understood the nuances of politics and diplomacy better than anyone. So it was surprising to President Wilson that Abdulaziz seemed rattled. Perspiration covered his forehead.

"Let me be frank," the ambassador began. "The threat from Shuhada' Alnnabi is growing at an alarming rate. The bombing in Riyadh gave them instant legitimacy as a terrorist organization. Thousands of young radicals are flocking to their cause. The *Mabahith* reports a major influx of students leaving school to join terrorist training camps in Afghanistan, Yemen, Syria, and other locations. They are building an army."

"Well," the president cut in, "I have no doubt that your secret police are accurate and let me assure you we are taking the Shuhada' Alnnabi threat very seriously. We want them neutralized as bad as you for the oil derrick bombings and the attack on OPEC. Also, I have spoken with my intelligence agencies and we have agreed to divulge classified Intel we think you will find useful."

Abdulaziz inched toward the end of his seat.

"Russia and China have been watching many of their training camps and are planning an attack," the president said. "We also are aware those nations funnel money to Shuhada' Alnnabi to destabilize Western interests. That leads us to believe a serious falling out has occurred because of these recent attacks. There may be new leadership in the shadows, a splinter cell, or a schism working under the Shuhada' Alnnabi name."

Ambassador Abdulaziz blinked. He waited a few seconds to make sure the president was done before saying, "Yes, Mr. President, we already have that intelligence."

"Oh."

"Let me also share something. The violence in Saudi Arabia escalates each day. We have suppressed reports or offered erroneous official accounts to downplay the terrorist threat. Shuhada' Alnnabi sees themselves as liberators and will not stop until they have the head of the king on a pike. So we do not advertise for their cause by reporting on such attacks but that does not mean the terrorists are not emboldened. We have seen twenty-four suicide bombers take out targets all over Saudi Arabia. None have been on the scale of the Riyadh shopping mall attack, which makes us believe that attack was the only one centrally planned and executed. These others were perpetrated by home-grown terrorists who are acting alone, or with minimal aid, in the name of Shuhada' Alnnabi."

The president cleared his throat. This was new information. All of a sudden he lost the upper hand. And that annoyed him. "Please convey my condolences to your King and the people of Saudi Arabia."

"Yes, yes I will do that. There is something else," the ambassador said with a noticeable level of reluctance.

"Oh?" *Dear God, what else?*

"There were six of our top men from our Ministry of Energy, Industry, and Mineral Resources killed in the Riyadh shopping mall attack. One was set to become the next cabinet secretary. He was one of our most brilliant minds and I cannot stress his importance. When he died the modernization of oil production was set back at least five years. The security cameras show the suicide bombing exploded a minute after he entered the main area. The terrorists targeted him."

"But they have not taken credit for the assassination? That seems odd." On the outside, the president was all business. But on the inside he wanted to scream. In his heart, Lloyd Wilson was still the same hippie who protested Vietnam and smoked ganja with his "choom gang." He never understood why people had to hurt each other in such ways.

"We have kept it out of the news and yes, it is odd, if it was their intention to kill him. Few people outside the upper echelon of our government understand how important a man he was to our entire industry. The terrorists did not care about publicizing his death because killing him was more important to their overall goal of spinning our top economic resource into total chaos. This was a targeted attack meant to cripple our oil production, and it has done immense damage."

"I see," the president said. He hated being so uninformed in a meeting with anyone, let alone a foreign dignitary. American intelligence services dropped the ball on this one.

"I am instructed," the ambassador continued, "by my government to formally ask for help. We need military advisors, weapons, and American special forces to find terrorist cells in the Middle East."

"We already do that. And rather effectively I might add."

"Yes, Mr. President, but we will allow your military to operate *inside* Saudi Arabia for the first time."

The president paused. He looked the ambassador right in the eye and sensed his desperation and shame. The country must be on the brink of total disaster. The American intelligence apparatus would never have predicted in a thousand years the tight-knit and closed society of Saudi Arabia would ask a foreign power, let alone the United States which was hated in many circles in the country, to bring in warriors to combat their own people. That would be like asking North Korea to send their Special Operation Force to find and destroy domestic terrorists in the hills of the Blue Ridge Mountains.

"An arms deal is one thing but sending in troops and military advisors is something I'm just not willing to commit. I will take it under advisement but I don't see how that will be possible."

"I understand your hesitancy, Mr. President. But these are dire times. If our government were ever to fall, then you would have another radicalized state in the Middle East more powerful than Iran. We would never make these claims if the situation was not untenable. For us to beg a foreign power for help is quite objectionable. But we must work together to end the terrorist threat once and for all."

The president stood and paced the room. Wilson rubbed his chin as the ambassador watched every move. "I need time for counsel and will be in touch. Thank you for coming in today."

The ambassador shook hands with President Wilson again and exited the Oval Office. The president's secretary entered and said, "You have a call from William Gladstone."

"Gladstone? Was this on my schedule?"

"No, sir, he just called."

"Okay, thanks."

President Wilson almost forgot about his troubling meeting with the Saudi Ambassador as he strode to his desk and picked up the phone.

"Bill, how are you?" The president asked.

The gruff voice on the other line replied, "Doing just well, Mr. President, thank you for taking my call."

"What do I owe the pleasure?"

"I have a few important matters to discuss."

"For you, Bill, anything. And I imagine this concerns information about the oil spill cleanup. I assure you, we are doing everything we can and I am confident the flow of oil into the Gulf will cease soon."

"I'm sure you have it well in hand. But that's not the reason for my call."

The president realized this was the second time today he was caught surprised.

"I am sure things will work out for the best and you'll be a stronger president for it, but I was hoping we might discuss the proposal we chatted about last month involving the national gas tax."

This again? "Yes, and while I'm with you on that I don't think it's the right time to introduce it in the middle of an energy crisis."

"It's exactly the right time!" Gladstone interjected. "A percentage-based tax would raise an incredible amount of revenue. Put that into clean energy development and your green agenda is funded for the next two decades."

"Hey, Bill, I get it. And I'd love to do that. But thanks to the political situation, it will be impossible to pass right now. The greatest ideas in the world cannot be sold to fickle voters. They vote with their wallets and right now they're more concerned with the costs of filling gas tanks in order to get to work or drop their kids off at school. I can't sell them on the greater good with that at the tops of their minds."

The other end of the line momentarily silenced. "Let me stop by later this week. There's something I'd like to show you that might change your mind. What do you say?"

The president wanted to slam the phone down. "Okay, Bill, I owe you that much." William Gladstone was not the type of man you hang up on. There was no one more connected and he had the ability to build or tear down a person on a whim.

"Great, I'll set it up with your secretary."

"Is there anything else I can do for you, Bill?"

"Actually the real reason for my call is to get back to you on your request for a recommendation to head the DNC next year."

"Oh, who do you think can handle that?"

"Senator Tom Mullen," William Gladstone replied.

CHAPTER 24

DINNER AT CUBA LIBRE IN THE heart of Washington, D.C., was normally a treat for Madison. She and John visited often. They ate late night after most of the crowds had left, otherwise they would inevitably run into someone who ruined their private evening. But the encounters with Fran Norris and Tom Mullen had Madison on edge. But that did not dissuade John from indulging.

"Another round of drinks!" John cheered to their waiter. Madison had not touched the Margarita sitting in front of her, but John failed to notice. Madison figured he must have had a good day on the stock market. Although there had been nothing but bad news recently, there are always winners in the financial sector. Madison could have asked for details, but she did not care.

John was crushing tortilla chips and guzzling drinks like it was his last meal. The big smile on his face symbolized his obliviousness to his wife's solemn mood. Madison's mind raced from one deep thought to another. "John," she said, "did I make a mistake running for office?"

John froze. Tortilla chip crumbs fell from his open mouth. "Why would you say that? Aren't you happy with what you've been able to accomplish?"

Madison rolled her eyes. "I've accomplished nothing. No bill of mine will even get a vote until I get through a few terms. That's the way it is in DC—they prioritize seniority over ideas and practicality."

John wiped his face with a napkin. "Maybe so, but this is what you were born to do. At least that's what I thought, no?"

"Everyone is in it for themselves," she said. "But that's not new information. If I didn't realize that in my childhood growing up with Dad playing the game then I never will. It seems that the major players are more interested in palace intrigue than getting things done to help the country. And I have to tell you, Boyd's death has made me reexamine a lot of different positions."

John took a long sip from his drink. "What do you mean?"

"I'm not sure it's worth it anymore."

"Oh come on! You can't be this jaded!" John rested his hand on top of Madison's. "Your political career just started! I know losing Boyd was a blow. Maddy, we can be distant sometimes because of our work but I still understand you. I won't pretend to have an explanation for why Boyd did what he did but he loved you like a daughter and more than that he believed in you."

"I know, but it's still my choice. Sometimes I think we would be better off leaving the public life behind and, I dunno, start a family."

John froze again. He stared into Madison's down-turned eyes until she glanced up. "I thought we closed the door on that a long time ago."

"Sometimes I don't know. I'm not sure about anything anymore. I'm having a crisis of conscience here."

"Well, let me ask you this: are you more frustrated because you believe nothing meaningful can get done or do you just hate the politics?"

"Both, I guess."

"Then I've got a solution." John sat back and grinned as if he had just solved the world's greatest problem. "Run for Boyd's senate seat."

Madison stared at John as if he had snails pouring out his ears. "What?" she said with a high-pitched voice. "Why would I ever want to do that?"

"Seniority isn't as important in the senate. I mean, it is, but you're not as anonymous when you're one of a hundred instead of one of four hundred and thirty-five. Plus it would give you meaning by carrying on Boyd's legacy."

"Yea, but Peter Baylor…"

John rolled his eyes and laughed. "Peter Baylor is a fool. You've told me that countless times. You'd be doing the people of Virginia a favor by knocking him out of the race."

"There are too many fools in DC. What would preventing one more from gaining office accomplish?"

"A lot. You can get more done and, hey, who knows, maybe someday you'll eye the big chair. The senate puts you in a better position."

Madison laughed. "John, no wonder I've made it this far. With a cheerleader like you, I probably could. But let me be clear on this; I have no desire for higher office. Ever. Period. I am not even sure I want to continue with the office I have now. And your solution is to run for something else? Come on. I'm more tempted to work toward bringing the whole system crashing down."

John shrugged and took another swig of his margarita. Madison poked at her plate with a fork until a chirping noise emitting from John's phone interrupted the moment.

"Uh-oh," he said. "Looks like I missed a call. That's odd, it didn't even ring."

John put his phone to his ear, removed it to enter his code, then listened intently. Madison watched as his smile faded. He looked down after about a minute then met Madison's eyes with concern.

"What?" she asked.

"You have to listen to this. And brace yourself."

John hit speaker and played back the voicemail.

"Hi, this is Jennie from The Newscycle with Reginald Goldsmith. I am calling to get a comment from your wife, Madison Gladstone, and book her for our show tomorrow night. We received word that her father, former Governor William Gladstone is planning to not only endorse Peter Baylor for Senate but also hit the campaign trail. We're hearing they have at least six events planned for the next two weeks. Since he was too sick to campaign for you and we wanted to see if you could give us an update on his health and your thoughts since he never campaigned for you, and as far as we can tell, never offered his endorsement. If you can call me back at your convenience that would be great. Thanks a bunch!"

Madison locked eyes with her shocked husband. "What the heck is that about?" he asked.

"Oh, Dad is always up to something. But you know what? I don't care. He can do whatever he wants."

Madison whipped out her phone and shot a text to Chief of Staff Jason Phillips, "Did you get a call from Reginald Goldsmith's people about this Peter Baylor endorsement from my dad?"

Within a minute, Jason replied, "He's doing what?!?!? I have heard nothing! Want me to check it out?"

"Yeah, do some research and see what you can find," she replied.

"That is so odd they would call you but not my staff," Madison said to John. Her husband just gaped like a toddler caught stealing a sweet.

Odd indeed. *What the hell else could go wrong?* Madison thought to herself.

CHAPTER 25

THE INVENTOR OF THE ALARM CLOCK must be a sadist. Despite last evenings activities and the extraordinary plans for the day, that was the first thought going through the pounding head of the man with the codename Adder. He pushed aside an empty bottle of tequila laying in his bed and reached over a sleeping prostitute, who did not mind the incessant blaring in the room, and shut off the alarm clock. Adder rubbed his temples and suppressed the strong urge to vomit as he inspected his hotel room. The walls were stained, carpets ripped, and the sheets smelled of mothballs and tequila—a deadly combination to the senses.

Yet, they were still cleaner than the woman lying face down next to him who happened to be snoring louder than a lumberjack. Adder exited the bed slowly and naked as the day he was born and reached for a large bottle of ibuprofen. He ached to pop a few Percocet, but he needed a clear mind today. Six ibuprofen would have to do. Adder labored to swallow the pills with a dry throat then turned to shake his night companion awake.

"Hey, time to go," he shouted. The short brunette groaned as she stirred and removed herself from the bed. Adder grabbed his wallet, removed a few bills and threw them on the bed. He took his wallet with him into the bathroom as he ran a shower. Adder gazed at his unshaven face and bloodshot eyes in the mirror before taking a long shower. He never felt clean enough no matter how much soap or scalding hot water he used. But that did not stop him from trying.

Adder turned off the water, dried himself and stood in front of the bathroom mirror once again. He opened his night bag and removed the razor and makeup kit. After a few minutes, he had a well-groomed but bushy mustache dyed black, along with the hair on his head, to hide the gray and age. Adder rubbed bronzer over his face and hands to resemble the look of a Latino.

Adder entered the bedroom to find his companion gone. He opened the closet and pulled out a capitán's uniform from the Bolivarian National Air Force of Venezuela. Adder dressed then returned once again to the bathroom. He looked the part, now the rest was up to him, his wits, and his training.

Adder glanced in the mirror again while fighting back tears. "Okay," he said. "You can do this. Just a few more jobs then we find a way out."

He was lying to himself, as he often did. But it helped get through these abominable missions. Adder cleaned the room before leaving. He wiped down anywhere he had touched to remove lingering fingerprints. He collected all of the trash and wrapped it in the bedsheets. Adder stuffed it into his suitcase with the rest of his belongings, opened the door to the room with a handkerchief, and entered the hallway.

Last night, Adder had stolen a military jeep from a group of drunken service members who would be too scared of retribution to report the theft. The drive to Base Aérea Francisco de Miranda was uneventful despite the poverty stricken beggars approaching at every stop. The streets were filled with military and police to prevent food riots and anti-government protests. He made only one stop, for five cups of coffee.

His arrival at the fortified base caused Adder no nervousness. Despite the outward appearance of a strong military machine in Venezuela, it was anything but. Soldiers were as fed up with the teetering government as everyone else. They would do their duty but bypassing what should be arduous military procedures was the easiest part of Adder's mission. Discipline broke down in most sectors years ago. But that did not mean Adder would lessen his resolve to get the job done. Any of these missions always had a low probability of success but his training and perseverance evened out ill chances. A part of him was proud of his deadly accomplishments but the overwhelming viewpoint of himself was nothing short of unadulterated loathing.

The guard glanced at Adder's fabricated identification. It was not the best reproduction of a government ID, but it was not bad. If a trained eye had examined it close enough, they would have noticed some distinct differences. Adder could have paid for some stolen IDs or for a better forger, and if this had been an American military base, he would have. But for Venezuela, mediocrity would do just fine. The guard gave Adder a lazy salute and opened the gate.

Adder drove to the farthest airfield at the base; the only one with any activity. He parked the jeep, grabbed the coffee, and jaunted over to a crew surrounding a B-52 bomber. The capitán of the plane was going over details of the training mission assignment as Adder approached. They stopped to look at him as he waved and said, "*Hola amigos.*"

Adder handed fabricated orders to the capitán and said in perfect Spanish, "With your permission, my superiors would like me to join your flight today. I will fly a B-52 at the Base Aérea Urdaneta starting next month and am instructed to watch your protocols."

"You are more than welcome," the burly capitán said to Adder as he read the orders.

"I bought coffee for everyone. Is it okay if I pass it out after we take off so it does not interfere?"

"Thank you Capitán, that is very generous."

"Please, continue your briefing. I would just like to look over the aircraft if you don't mind."

"Absolutely."

Adder circled the B-52, trying to appear like he was making a lackadaisical inspection of the aircraft. He returned to hear the final orders confirming phony orders issued to munitions were successful.

"We are also carrying napalm bombs today."

Adder smiled.

The flight plan comprised a short trip to the border of Venezuela and back. The takeoff went smoothly, and it was not long before Adder was passing out coffee to the radar navigator and the electronics warfare officer. The crew settled in for the flight, laughing and carousing with Adder. They told stories about family and were loose with details surrounding past missions. The laughter brought back the copilot who joined in on the fun. Adder made sure he received a cup of coffee.

"So," Adder explained, "If you want a good woman then you need to make sure she can talk for hours."

The crew laughed. The copilot asked, "Why would you ever want that?"

"Because," Adder continued while trying to suppress his own laughter, "the only way to prevent a woman from getting mad is to not say anything at all. It's better to let her say whatever she wants as much as she wants than for you to say something, which she will think is stupid anyway."

They all laughed hysterically before the radar navigator coughed. The copilot slapped his back in a joking manner. But then the navigator's face turned blue as he gasped for air.

"Laughing too hard, *amigo*?" Adder said with a big smile.

The rest of the crew silenced as the navigator made wheezing noises and fell to his knees. "He's having a heart attack!" the copilot yelled.

They laid him on the floor of the plane. The electronics warfare officer ran for the first-aid kit. "I need to get the capitán to turn around," the copilot yelled as he stood and made his way for the cockpit. "No, no," Adder said, "You must stay and keep him comfortable. I will tell the capitán, stay here, please *amigo*." The copilot nodded and held the navigator as he convulsed.

Adder headed to the cockpit. "May I come in?" he asked the pilot as he slid on an aviation headset. The pilot waved him in as Adder sat down in the copilot's chair.

"So," Adder asked. "Where are we?"

"We are just coming up on the Orinoco Belt in Boyaca. You will see the tar fields for miles from up here."

"Ah, yes, the belt," Adder replied. "That is the key to our country's wealth is it not? Hundreds of millions of barrels of oil are located in those fields."

"I suppose. I know little of such things."

Adder nodded. "Listen, *amigo,* when we get above Boyaca I want you to turn East and continue toward the coast."

The pilot glance at him with a frown. "What? Why would I do that?"

"It's our orders. Our superiors ordered this course correction. You will do it."

"I will not!" The pilot said. "I have no such orders." He sternly turned away from Adder to gaze out the dashboard window.

Adder shook his head, removed a pistol from his coat pocket, pointed it at the pilot, and pulled the trigger. With a ringing in his ears from the gunshot Adder quickly took over the controls and made the course correction himself. He then turned on the autopilot as he saw the Orinoco Belt approaching. Adder stood and made his way to the back of the plane where the rest of the crew lay dead from the poison in the coffee.

The brutal assassin then took the seat normally occupied by the electronic warfare officer. He had trained extensively for this moment. The keypad and controls were a perfect match to the dummy controls he practiced with for months. In a few clicks, the bomb bay doors opened. With another flick of a switch the payload of napalm dropped. The oil fields erupted. The bombing run would not destroy the entire 25,000 kilometer belt, but it would do more than enough damage for Adder's employers' purposes. It would take weeks to put out the fires. Smoke would be seen for miles.

Adder removed a small GPS tracker from his pocket. The beacon on the device blinked on a location about five miles out to sea. Within no time at all, the plane made its way unmolested to the coast and beyond. The Venezuelan military was still trying to react to what had just happened. No jets were scrambled to take down the B-52. Adder counted on this. The second-rate Venezuelan military command would spin the blame on anti-government rebels or the Americans. All the while, there was plenty of time to escape.

When the GPS beacon showed the plane above the predetermined spot, Adder jumped from the bomb bay doors. He parachuted into the water close to where his sailboat waited, anchored in the middle of nowhere. Adder removed the parachute and swam to the boat. In a few hours, he would be in Miami and onto the next mission. The B-52 would crash in the middle of the ocean when it ran out of fuel. Adder had removed the black box and destroyed the tracking systems. The Venezuelans may still find the plane but it was unlikely. If they did, there would be no embarrassing report of a murdered crew.

Adder would need to find another bottle of tequila before the day was over.

CHAPTER 26

PRESIDENT WILSON FELT THE ENERGY FROM the Ohio crowd in his entire body. He had many dark days in his presidency but rallies like this made it all worthwhile. When he saw the hope in the eyes of his biggest supporters, he knew he was on the right track. The high school auditorium was packed with students, longtime Democrats, and local union workers. The media stationed in the back would undoubtedly paint this rally a huge success. Wilson would record this moment in his memoirs as the turning point in his administration when America lined up behind him once again. Together, perhaps, they would forge a path forward that would result in one of the most loved and successful presidencies.

The president knew this line of thinking was borderline arrogant. But he also accepted that it was essential to view his role in society in such a way. The American people needed a strong leader. And after a persuasive talk with William Gladstone, he was energized to push bold reforms in the moment of national crisis. Gas prices exploded past $6 a gallon after the Orinoco Belt accident. He was still skeptical that one of their planes could misplace a practice bombing run so badly, but he accepted it for the time being, and would not let a crisis go to waste.

The crowd was on their feet. Wilson used their liveliness to punctuate every line of his speech with enthusiasm. He was a master of using mannerisms to achieve desired reactions. The president described it as making love to the crowd. Every action had a proper reaction. After thirty minutes of hitting on just about everything the crowd wanted to hear, he was prepared to deliver the final elements of his new energy plan that would be the center-piece of the news cycle for the next forty-eight hours— more than enough time to jumpstart these policy initiatives on Capitol Hill.

"And with bold action, we will radically alter the distri-bution and consumption of energy in the United States," Wilson said to an ever increasingly energetic crowd. "This is the beginning. Right now, right here. No longer will we stand powerless to stop sea levels from rising. No longer will pollution poison our skies and waterways. Climate change will stop in its tracks and no longer will we fear for the lives of our children. We will give them a real promise of a clean tomorrow."

The crowd ate up every word. Wilson was on a roll.

"To live this dream, you and I must act now. The oil companies are in the midst of the most horrific price gouging the world has ever witnessed. They are using tragedy to raise prices and fill their pockets so they can buy more polluting corporate jets and homes the size of small cities. It is time they acknowledge their crimes against humanity and the destructive force of their deadly product. And if they do not, I have instructed my Department of Justice to look into options for prosecution of oil executives. I have also given orders to the Environmental Protection Agency to institute new regulations that will handcuff the entire industry and force them into the twenty-first century line of thinking regarding clean energy and renewable resources.

"Because that's the only way we can move forward as a nation. Our future will be powered by wind, solar, hydro-electric, and other sustainable methods. Our children will not know a planet in peril. They won't need to fork over large portions of their paychecks to oil companies just to fill their tanks to get to work. It will be glorious but it will be difficult. Ladies and gentlemen, it's time for a little tough love.

"The oil industry and my political opposition refuse to get in line. So it is up to us to make them see the truth. That is why I will issue an executive order to release every barrel in the strategic oil reserves. I will also push for the complete dissolution of the program. No longer will the government of the United States horde oil. We will not rely on that filth to fuel our economy. Sustainable energy sources will power government buildings, vehicles, and yes, even the military. This push will not be easy and sure, we could wait a few decades and introduce these reforms piecemeal, but that's not how you get things done with the planet near death. We will become energy independent and rely on green technologies within ten years.

"And I know what you're thinking. You think, Lloyd, this sounds great and all but there will still be dinosaurs in the coal and oil industry that will fight tooth and nail to stop you. And you are right. They are not going to accept reality. So, again, it's time to give them even more tough love. I will send to Congress a bill outlining a new carbon tax and a cap-and-trade system. And guess what? I still know what you're thinking. You're thinking, great, another way for Congress to take money and put it toward pet projects and return political favors. Trust me, I'm as sick of this practice as you are. So one hundred percent of the revenue raised from these new taxes will go into research and development of green technologies and to modernize and shift the energy sector toward sustainability. And that's it. There will be no skimming off the top. There won't be

massive amounts of 'administrative costs' that really mean
kickbacks to corrupt officials. No, this is real folks. And it's
happening now.

"But I can't do this alone. Your friends and neighbors
will hear the lies peddled by Big Oil and Big Coal. They
will tell you, 'President Wilson just wants to raise taxes and
hurt the economy.' And that's when I need you to get in
their face and say, 'No, that's not accurate at all. President
Wilson is modernizing the economy so we can all share
in the prosperity of the American dream. A carbon tax is
the only way for 'Big Oil' to pay for the damage they have
done to the planet. The release of carbon dioxide into the
atmosphere is killing us. Forcing them to pay penalties is
the incentive needed to make them *voluntarily* move away
from destructive practices. Together, we will end the oil
and coal industries!

"Now, with gas prices so high they will say this is the
worst time for a carbon tax. And I was one of those people
as well until I sat down with a good friend of mine who
explained that this is the perfect time. We will raise so
much revenue for clean energy it will only take months,
maybe a few years, before we have enough funding for
decades to come. And hey, if it puts a few oil companies
out of business then who cares right?"

The crowd jumped up and down in excitement. Many
had tears in their eyes. This was the speech they were waiting
to hear from an American president. The audience could
feel change coming. Real change. Not the stuff you hear in
a normal political speech that ends up with no results. The
crowd shook with energy infusing their very souls.

This would be epic. Their dreams were becoming
a reality and no one would dare oppose this plan. The
message was transcendental. The resisters would be few

because the American people would know those people were only in it for themselves.

It was inspiring, earth shattering, and really going to happen, they all thought.

CHAPTER 27

"IT WAS A COMPLETE JOKE," REP. Fran Norris told Reginald Goldsmith with her most somber face. Goldsmith was interviewing Fran in-studio the day after President Wilson's rally. The media called it the "tough love" speech, and many already deemed it a massive miscalculation by the president. Even some of his most ardent supporters jumped ship. His opposition smelled blood, and they were ready to pounce.

"The fact of the matter is the president thinks we're all stupid," Norris continued. "He had the gall to say our energy sector is going to 'voluntarily' move away from coal and oil. That is outrageous. He's putting a gun to their heads! This is a war on coal and oil. And where does he get off thinking the perfect time to push the largest tax increase in the history of the country is with gas over $6 a gallon? Come on."

Reginald Goldsmith sat cross-legged across from Norris with his head resting on his hand. He wore his wide-frame glasses to appear more intellectual, a common tactic amongst news people. Many accused Goldsmith of blatant bias and favoritism toward leftist causes, and his personal opinions swayed that way, but in reality he was an opportunist and a populist. Goldsmith was not stupid enough to ally himself with fruitless endeavors and lack-luster moral crusades.

"That's tough talk," he replied, barely moving. He kept a rigid posture to portray control of the situation. "But I don't think you're off base here. Our snap poll shows that approval of the president's new tax plan sits at 14 percent. And while he has time to build on that, it's a tough mountain to climb. Tell me, what would your advice be to President Wilson?"

"What advice could I give?" Norris said with a mock laughter. "He's dug a hole and I don't think he possesses the intelligence to dig himself out of it right now. If he drops support for his plan, he looks weak. If he continues to insist on this massive tax increase, and by all accounts he is, I saw the announcement out of the White House that he will be traveling the country to push this plan in coming weeks, then he will be embarrassed on a national scale. Congress won't get behind this. How are we supposed to back a major tax hike then go back and explain that to our constituents who can barely afford to fill their tanks? It's ludicrous."

"So, I take it these measures are dead on arrival on the Hill?"

"Oh, absolutely. There's little chance of this getting passed. The current Congress is close to the middle ideologically. Pushing a tax increase this big would indicate a major lurch leftward. And I don't think even my Democratic friends are willing to make that move."

"So, where is this coming from?" Goldsmith repositioned to another one of his intellectual poses. "The president never campaigned on environmental issues as a candidate. There was no discussion of a Carbon Tax or a war on oil and coal. What do you think is motivating him to make this move now amid an energy crisis?"

"It's simple, Reginald. The president has completely and utterly cracked under the pressure. He has been punched in the mouth with this national crisis and he has no way to punch back. He has gotten some terrible advice or has, I don't know, snapped, I guess."

"Bold words. So the president is up for reelection next year. The primaries begin in early January. Do you think someone from his own party will mount a challenge? His approval ratings continue to tank. If this keeps up, he's looking at going into an election year with 30 percent of the population backing him, maybe less. Can he recover?"

"I have seen some incredible comeback stories in politics at every level. Whenever you count anyone out, sometimes, they surprise you. So it's hard for me to say someone is completely finished, especially an incumbent president. But this is as close to being done as possible. The voting populace is fickle. They forget a speech as offensive as what we heard yesterday over a matter of time. And rightfully so, the American people are busy living their lives. They don't have time to immerse themselves in politics like we do up on the Hill. But I tell you, whenever they fill their tanks for $6, $7 a gallon, they will remember their president tried to gouge them even further.

"And to answer your question about a primary challenge I think that's near to impossible even with his unpopularity. Challenging a sitting president is political suicide. Just ask Pat Buchanan. He not only sank his own chances for a future political career but he robbed the Republican Party of beating Bill Clinton four years later. And George H. W. Bush was not losing popularity nearly as fast as Lloyd Wilson!"

"So there's no chance?"

"Look, someone may challenge him but there probably isn't anyone who could mount a reputable campaign. And if they want to run later down the road, their chance will be ruined. But why are you asking me about Democratic politics? I'm more concerned with making sure the nominee of my party is ready to take down Lloyd Wilson."

"So are you leaning toward one candidate or another?"

"It's too early for that. No one has officially announced. But I will tell you, if anyone was on the fence two days ago, they're committed now. They should be licking their lips in anticipation of taking on Wilson."

"And what about you? Would you ever consider running?"

Fran Norris burst out laughing. "I know better, Reginald, don't even try that."

"That's not a denial."

"You're right. So let me be clear. There's zero chance I will run for president. But I want to see someone qualified and ready to take over on day one. I will watch every candidate or potential candidate very closely."

CHAPTER 28

"THIS DOESN'T SEEM LIKE POLITICS AS usual," Madison said to Special Agent Walter Robinson. After a few days of contemplating the run-in with Fran Norris, Madison phoned Walter. "Although, some of the oddest things happen up on the Hill."

"That's true," Robinson said with a mock laugh. "I can look into Fran Norris and Tom Mullen for any connections with Senator Radford."

"That would be good but nothing may come from it."

"Something is off, for sure. I don't presume to be a seasoned political operative but why is a Republican meddling with Democratic politics so much? And why would fellow Democrats work with a Republican to mount a primary challenge against the president?"

"It's not unheard of," Madison replied, "but discussions are never made publicly. The power structures in DC differ greatly from what the average American assumes. But this is somewhat unusual. There seems to be an orchestrated plot to get me to drop this whole thing, and it is not unlike the pressure you're receiving. Perhaps I'm being paranoid because I desperately want an explanation for Boyd's suicide."

"Hey, listen," Agent Robinson said with an emphatic tone, "I think you may have stumbled onto something here bigger than we both assumed. Let me do some digging and circle back. In the meantime, what can you do on your end?"

"Well, I've got personal business to attend, but it may also give us some answers."

"Anything I can help with?"

"I'm not even sure I can help myself. But thanks. I'll be in touch."

CHAPTER 29

ALTHOUGH MADISON FEARED THE DESTINATION, THE drive through Stanley, Virginia, was a breath of fresh air. Surrounded by majestic mountains and nonexistent traffic, almost anyone embedded in D.C. could find tranquility. She drove through a heavily wooded area, with houses ranging from mansions to starter homes stationed sporadically. Madison turned on an unmarked road and drove three miles until the pavement turned to gravel. There were no houses in sight, just trees, bushes, and the occasional deer.

Madison continued to the end of the road where a long and narrow driveway hid her destination behind lush foliage. A gate blocked the entrance. Next to the gate was a small shack where an armed man in a security uniform emerged and beckoned her to stop. Madison rolled down the car window as the guard approached and bent down.

"Oh, hi, Mrs. Gladstone, how are you today?"

"I'm well, Jimmy. Could you please open the gate?"

Jimmy hesitated and cleared his throat while shifting his eyes up and down the car. "Uh, one second, okay?"

Madison sighed then said, "You've got to be kidding me," under her breath as Jimmy retreated to the guard shack and picked up the phone. His whispered conversation took much longer than Madison expected before he pressed a button to open the gates. He hung up the phone and waved Madison on, who gave a sarcastic smile and wave as she sped up the long mountain road.

The two-mile-long hike put Madison at the top of a ridge where a massive home overlooked the entire valley. The picturesque plantation-style mansion boasted long windy porches stretching around the front and both sides on each level of the five-level home. The painted white columns surrounded the front like soldiers standing at attention. And while it appeared like something predominant in the 1800s, inside it had all the modern conveniences imaginable. Like its inhabitant, it portrayed a facade to hide its true nature.

A maid stood on the porch with her hands respectfully crossed across her lap as she awaited Madison to park in the circle in front of the house. A massive fountain with detailed architectural design centered the circle of the driveway. Madison parked, exited the vehicle, and approached the maid. "Come right this way, please," she said robotically, beckoning Madison to follow.

The maid led her into an elegant study filled with two levels of bookcases surrounding the entire room. It smelled of leather and old paper with a hint of lilac from whatever cleaning products the janitorial staff used. Many of the ancient books were more for decoration and rarely ever removed but there was not a speck of dust in the entire room. The library was large enough to house a good-sized party of at least a hundred people. Three simple black leather couches sat in the middle of the room facing each other in an open square. The maid invited Madison to make herself comfortable and offered a drink, to which Madison politely declined. The maid curtsied and left the room.

After ten minutes of impatience, Madison pulled out her phone and fingered through emails and messages. Madison was wading through her upcoming schedule when a familiar gruff voice said, "Hello, Maddy. I wasn't expecting you."

Madison put the phone down and replied, "Hello, Dad."

William Gladstone was an imposing figure in the political world. He stood over six feet tall, almost never flubbed a line, and was quick to throw out impressive facts during debates and interviews that no one saw coming. The media loved William, often giving him a free pass to do and say anything. The people of Virginia held him in higher regard. Although much time had passed since leaving office, many political figures still sought him for counsel, endorsements, and fundraising appeals. But as legendary as William Gladstone the politician was, he was a tough nut to crack as a man. And that is why Madison was not looking forward to this conversation.

"It's been a long time since I've heard from you, Maddy. How is John?"

"He's good, Dad. How's your health?"

"Nothing can slow me down," William said with a wink.

William Gladstone sat on a couch opposite to Madison. He wore a long wool robe over silk pajamas and brown leather slippers free from scuffs or wear and tear. His retro browline glasses complemented his salt-and-pepper hair, short, and parted to the right. Even in pajamas, William Gladstone looked the part of the consummate politician.

"So what brings you here?"

Madison took a deep breath. "Last time we talked it did not end well. And I'm sorry things got so heated."

"Me too."

Madison paused to summon her strength. "I didn't understand your refusal to back my candidacy. It hurt. I still don't get it."

William Gladstone adjusted his glasses, crossed his legs, and leaned back on the sofa. Madison experienced the gaze of an adoring father for a fleeting moment as it quickly melted back to the stone-faced politician. "We've been over this," he scolded. "I realize things have been tense between us since your mother died."

"Things have been that way between us forever," Madison interjected.

William Gladstone smoothed his robe. "Be that as it may you have to understand that I want nothing but the best for you. I created a pathway for your ascendance into public life. You were perfectly set up to run for governor and it would have been a cakewalk. Executive experience is the pathway to the senate, the White House, or an ambassadorship or something greater. The House of Representatives is almost always a pit to nowhere."

Madison shook her head. This was as well as any conversation went with her father. It was not until she reached her late teenage years that she learned how to fight back. "But it's a chance to do something for the people of my district," Madison tried to hold back her angst in her voice. "That's all I ever wanted. To make our home a little bit better. I want none of those things you mentioned. This is about me and my path, not yours."

William Gladstone turned his head a notch and looked his daughter up and down as if for the first time. "I respect that."

Madison almost choked saying, "What?" But the euphoria didn't last long.

"But you have to respect that I've been in this business a long time and my opinion matters. No, it's not even an opinion, it's a *fact*. I deal in *facts*. And it's a *fact* we have the makings of a political dynasty. Your grandfather blazed the trail for me in the senate and I did the same for you in the governor's mansion. You can reject all the sacrifices I made for you, that's your right as an American, but that doesn't mean I have to approve." William Gladstone crossed his arms.

"Screw your political dynasty, Dad."

"Watch your mouth!" William's face heated.

Madison forced her father to show emotion. That was a rare feat indeed. Now it was time to catch him off guard if she was ever going to get anywhere. "Why are you endorsing Peter Baylor?"

The trick failed as William Gladstone did not skip a beat. In public or private, he never showed any sign of being unprepared or rattled. To voters that was an admirable quality. To Madison though, it was agonizing. "Politics," he replied coolly.

"And politics was the reason you couldn't endorse me?"

"Yes."

"See," Madison huffed as she stood and pointed violently at her father. "That's why you and I will never be on the same page. It wasn't ever about politics; it was about family. Why you still don't understand that is incomprehensible."

Madison marched toward the door. Her father said nothing. She winced after a moment of realization. She almost left before meeting the objective of the visit. But the pain of having to turn and face her father one last time was almost too much. He stared at the ground as she gazed at him. He never seemed so frail. It was a rare moment of weakness for such a titan.

"This is not how I wanted this to go," she said. "I came here to ask you something. I've been working with the FBI on Boyd's death."

William Gladstone met her eyes again but showed no sign of surprise.

Madison continued, "You and Boyd had a big fight right before I announced that I was running for Congress. I always assumed it was about you disagreeing with my run."

William Gladstone nodded.

"But Boyd's wife, Jeanne, told me you two were working on something big together. She indicated that had as much to do with the fight as anything else."

"Oh?"

"What was that deal about? She said it had something to do with Senator Tom Mullen and Representative Fran Norris."

William Gladstone smiled thinly. "Nothing out of the ordinary I can assure you. We were considering the purchase of a local business."

"That's it?"

"That's it."

"Ok, but..."

"I don't mean to cut you off but I have an important phone call in about two minutes. I'm sorry, but Esmeralda will show you out."

William Gladstone stood and shuffled out the library as the maid arrived to escort Madison.

Madison was as confused as ever.

CHAPTER 30

MADISON RETURNED TO CAPITOL HILL THE day after meeting with her father with as much calm as possible given the circumstances. Something was still off and she could not shake the sensation that everyone else aside from her was in on some sick joke. Despite what William Gladstone thought she had good political instincts. The feeling of getting played was as powerful as ever, but there was no choice but to move forward.

Madison entered her outer office with a scowl. Jason Phillips perked up from his desk at the sound of the door. When their faces met, Madison realized something was wrong. Jason's normally bright demeanor transformed to serious chief-of-staff mode in an instant. "Morning, Congresswoman," he said.

"Hi, Jason. What's on tap for today?"

"Well, um, there is an unscheduled appointment waiting in your office."

Madison swelled, ready to rage. "Jason, you know better than to—"

"I get it," Jason interrupted, "but it's a man from the FBI."

Madison nodded. Walter Robinson might have found something. Good. That could be useful unless he is still harassing her for clues. Madison took a deep breath and opened the door to her inner office.

Sitting in a visitor chair was a familiar, frumpy-looking man. By the time he turned to face her, she remembered their initial meeting underneath the Capitol so many weeks ago with Fran Norris.

"Well, I didn't expect to see you ever again, aren't you in the CIA?"

"That would not be entirely inaccurate," the frumpy man said.

"So, why are you waving around FBI credentials?"

"I have found that people instantly respect the FBI. Intelligence agencies put people on the defensive soon after a confrontation. Everyone lets the FBI do whatever they want. Well, regular people anyway. Elected officials treat them like valets or punching bags. The Bureau and I have an understanding and they were gracious enough to issue credentials."

Madison took a seat behind her desk and removed her jacket, placing it on the back of the chair. The man wore the same used-up suit he wore during the intelligence briefing. "I did not catch your name," she replied as dignified as possible.

"George," he replied.

"George what?"

"Just George is fine."

"Don't be ridiculous. What is this—some dime-store novel? Even James Bond used a last name."

George raised an eyebrow. "Everyone I work with on the Hill knows me as George. And that's the way I'd like to keep it. Let me offer some background. In the eyes of the United States of America, I do not exist. You are not supposed to meet people like me until you've been through a few terms. Even then, only after you're put on certain committees. This is not something I take lightly. And for your information, I have never met with someone in their freshman year in Congress—never. While that might not mean much to you, it means a lot to me. I am one of the hundred people or so who really protects this country. And I have already said more than I would care to share with even the most senior-elected officials in this building."

Madison paused. This man lied for a living. Everything he said should be accepted with a level of skepticism. But that did not mean he was wrong.

"So why am I so special to receive a personal audience?" she asked.

"In that intelligence briefing, you showed real brass. And I've been around long enough to differentiate veiled arrogance from the genuine article. Some congressmen will speak up only to showboat, even in a closed door intelligence briefing or committee hearing. I see right through pomposity. But you seem willing to push politics aside for the good of this country. I have the unenviable task of greasing Capitol Hill enough so *my guys* can get what they need to make sure America is always at the forefront of fighting terror. I need people like you in my corner and I think you need people like me."

"Well, I'm flattered," Madison said flatly.

"Enough with the pleasantries," George said, sitting up straight. He went from rumpled vagabond to a seasoned bureaucrat in a split second. "There is something I want to divulge that someone with such limited experience as an elected official should never hear. But there are no written rules on what classified material can be shared with members of Congress. There has always been a 'need to know' basis. But the reality of this situation is you don't need to know. I only want you to because I see you as someone who can get things done."

"I don't know."

"I do," George interrupted. "Trust me. What I'm about to say must remain in the utmost confidence between us. You don't disclose this knowledge to anyone without my express permission. Most people in that intelligence briefing are not, nor will they ever be, privy to this information. But once you are made aware, there is no going back. And I won't sugarcoat it for you, it is disturbing. After a while you will accept it but your perspective on national security will change forever. Someday you will be running this place and the quicker you learn about this, the more time you will have for processing, and eventually learn to use it to your advantage."

Madison shot out of her chair and paced back and forth. "This is not something I won't take seriously."

"That's why I'm here."

On the inside Madison panicked. Boyd, her father, and the FBI investigation became an afterthought. George studied her as she sat once again and braced for impact. There had always been hints on the Hill of things like this where the deepest, darkest secrets of the Republic were weighed and discussed with decisions arising from those meetings affecting national policy for decades. But those were the conversations held amongst heads of state and the leadership, not with a freshman in Congress. Madison was unsure if she was ready to take on that responsibility. But this was why she was here, was it not?

"Ok, lay it on me," she said.

CHAPTER 31

JASON PHILLIPS WAS NO EAVESDROPPER. CONVERSATIONS amongst the power brokers should remain in confidence lest you desire to be drawn into their madness. Truthfully, if he was uninvited, he had no wish to be involved. The cesspool of Capitol Hill kept him busy enough. And while being the chief of staff of a congresswoman was like a cross between a janitor and a robot, he wanted to keep his position as long as sanity would allow.

If he had been eavesdropping, he could have barely made out a few words spoken behind the closed door of his boss as she met with the FBI agent. But for the last ten minutes it had been almost silent. Whatever they discussed was done quietly and without heavy reactions. Jason found himself inching his chair closer to the wall that divided Madison's office with his own desk.

Jason kicked back to a seated position and furiously typed gibberish on his computer as the door opened to Madison's office and the FBI agent exploded out and through the outer doors without so much as a head nod.

Jason stood and entered Madison's office. The congresswoman sat behind her desk staring out the window at nothing in particular with a pale face.

"Congresswoman, are you okay?"

Madison said nothing.

Jason waited a minute before saying, "Madison?"

She turned to him with glossy eyes. Madison had only looked so vulnerable once before—when she learned about Boyd Radford's suicide.

"I'm sorry, Jason," she said, emotionless. "Cancel my appointments today. I need a drink."

"What? It's nine o'clock in the morning." Jason said.

"Yea, it's a good time to get started."

"So, you're blowing off the day to go drinking?"

"Yep."

"Should I tell your canceled appointments that?"

"I don't care what you tell them."

Jason groaned.

CHAPTER 32

MADISON SAT AT THE SMALL WET bar in her townhome basement. She considered going to a real bar but only the seediest were open at this hour and a picture floating around social media of her shirking responsibilities to go drinking would be disastrous. Despite her current lack of emotion, Madison was not ready to throw everything away. Not yet anyway. Besides, there was plenty of booze in the comfort of her home. She poured another finger of Wasmund's Single Malt Whisky and knocked it to the back of her throat. The warmth greeted her like an old friend.

John exited his basement office and stopped dead. Madison did not need to turn to confirm his shocked face.

"Maddy, what the heck are you doing here drinking whisky this early in the morning?"

Madison did not respond. Instead, she pulled out the adjacent barstool and patted the seat. John approached and sat as Madison poured another drink and grabbed a glass for John. "It's a bit too early for me," he protested.

"Shut up and have a drink with your adoring wife. Pretend we're back in our college days, pre-gaming for football."

John laughed uncomfortably. "That was a long time ago, dear. But I have not become a total prude." John accepted the glass from Madison as she poured him a healthy amount.

"What's wrong?" he said with concern, leaning on his arm to face Madison.

She moved her glass in a circle with her thumb and index finger. Without meeting John's eyes, she said, "Sometimes I don't think what I'm doing is worth it. Maybe I should go work as a flight attendant or a waitress or something. At least that would be honest work."

John laughed. "Are you serious?" Madison shot him a look of disgust.

"I am, John. This job is not what I thought it would be. No, that's a lie. It's *exactly* what I thought it would be but had hoped it wouldn't. Does that make sense?"

"The aura of elected politics has lifted and you've discovered the job is too bureaucratic or so filled with phonies you can't stand the bogusness?"

Madison smiled and raised her glass to John who promptly clinked her cup with his. "John, you are one insightful man. Not totally accurate, but damn close. I knew I married you for a reason."

John laughed again. "I had been wondering about that. But if that's not it, what's the matter?"

"That's the thing. It's my burden to bear. I couldn't tell you even if I wanted to, but, I'd rather have no one share my anguish."

"Okay, I understand there are things you can't discuss. But if you need someone to get your mind off of things, I'm your man. I hope you don't expect me to get snockered every morning during workdays."

Madison chuckled and took another sip.

"So, how is your father?" John asked.

Madison stared at the bottom of her glass. She did not tell John about her meeting with her dad. Not that she was not trying to hide the visit; Madison just did not want to discuss it with anyone.

"I, uh, I don't…" she said before John cut in.

"I think it's time you forgave him."

"What?" she almost screamed.

"I recognize that seems odd for me to say."

"John, he said you were not the right match for me to your *face*! On our *wedding day*!"

John scratched his head. "Well… that was a long time ago. And family is family. Perhaps it's time to let things go and move on. I think that might make you a happier person. And honestly, that's all I care about. I love you, Maddy. And you will do extraordinary things, soon in fact, and he could be an ally."

"What things?"

"Hmm?"

"You said I will do 'extraordinary things, soon'—what did you mean by that?"

"Well… you're in Congress. There is a lot on your plate but you have a lot of great ideas and the ability to make them into reality."

"Ah, I see," Madison said, slurring. "You would make a great politician with that non-answer, John."

John showed no expression.

"But whatever. You need to get back to work, and I need to get back to this bottle. So move that cute little tush of yours back to work and then join me for a vodka lunch later on."

"Oh, dear. Take it easy, won't you?"

"Not today, John. Not today."

CHAPTER 33

MADISON AWOKE TO HER HEAD POUNDING. The incessant ringing from her cellphone felt like a jackhammer on her brain. John was already out of bed and at work. The clock read 5:00 a.m.. *Oh come on*, she thought, ignoring the phone, and letting the call go to voicemail. Her increasingly troublesome headache prevented her from falling back to sleep. Staring at the ceiling, she tried to keep down the stewing bile. Madison began to regret having drunk that entire bottle of Wasmund's.

The phone rang again. Madison grabbed John's pillow, put it to her face, and mockingly beat it to drown the ringing. But it rang again almost immediately. Madison groaned, stumbling through miscellaneous items on the side table until she located the phone. With her eyes closed she answered and put it to her ear. Madison rested her arm over her forehead.

"Hello?" she said groggily.

"Madison! Thank God. I need you right now," the distressed voice of Walter Robinson said on the other line. Walter's frantic pace made her alert.

"What is it? Did you find something?"

"Well, you could say that. How quickly can you be downstairs? I'm just pulling up to your house right now."

"You're what? Do you know what time it is?"

"You have to trust me. If you don't hurry, we will miss it. It's now or never."

"Miss what? What the hell are you talking about, Walt?"

"I'll explain in the car. Just come down."

"Okay, give me fifteen minutes."

"…Really?"

"Yes. And be thankful that a woman can get ready to go out in fifteen minutes, dammit."

CHAPTER 34

TWENTY MINUTES LATER MADISON EXITED HER front door to see Walter Robinson frantically bobbing back and forth in the front of his black BMW M3. The car was in drive and he motioned to get in fast. Madison was proud of the fact she looked almost presentable given the circumstances. There was little time for much makeup but her clothes were pristine and hair in order. She sprayed more perfume than usual to hide the stench of liquor that must be oozing out of her skin. Madison hoped she did not smell like a distillery.

Madison entered the car and before she could secure her seatbelt Walter sped off. "Whoa, slow down," she said. "I'm still trying to wake up and the five ibuprofen I swallowed will need time to kick in."

"I'm sorry," Walter said as he sped through her neighborhood and off toward the beltway. "We don't have a lot of time before we miss it."

"Ok, hold on," Madison said, irritated. "You rip me out of bed, don't give me any reason, and speed off like you robbed a bank. Tell me something or I may report you for kidnapping."

Walter cracked the hint of a smile. "You're right. I'm sorry and I realize this is unorthodox. But you remember how I was looking into Fran Norris and Tom Mullen?"

"Yeah."

"Well, I found something. Big. And I have to show it to you. And, well, maybe I should not say this, but, I tapped their phones."

Madison's eyes widened. "You did what? How did you get that approved? It's darn easy to get phones tapped on regular Americans but elected officials? Who do you know you can pull that off?"

Walter said nothing.

"Oh, you have got to be kidding me," she said covering her face with her hands. "What have you gotten me involved in? I can't be a part of this."

"You are a part of this. More than you think. Plus I am ready to risk everything over what I may have discovered. And there are bigger things to worry about than me being fired or prosecuted. Trust me."

Now it was Madison's turn to be silent. A million thoughts ran through her pulsating head. She kept quiet while Walter pulled his car to a nondescript row of offices in Arlington. He parked the car on a side street with a plain view of an office building a block away.

Walter glanced at the clock in his car, it read 5:29. "Okay, just wait a few minutes and watch that office up ahead." He pointed straight out the front window.

A big gray commercial sized truck pulled to the curb aside from the office. The logo on the side read, "Protect-U Shredding." A uniformed man exited the truck and entered the office.

"What am I looking at, Walter?"

"Just wait. And keep your eyes on the truck."

"What's so important about this truck? We use this company on the Hill. They take sealed trash cans of documents we want destroyed and shred them. It seems kind of silly that we can't do that ourselves, but whatever."

Walter met her eyes and shook his head.

"What?"

Before he could answer, the uniformed man exited the building with a giant sealed trash can with the same "Protect-U Shredding" logo. He wheeled it to the back of the truck where he opened the door and lifted the can into the truck. He shut the door, locked it, and made his way to the driver's seat.

Walter Robinson started up his BMW. He waited five seconds then followed the truck.

"Why are we following this truck? And what does this have to do with Fran Norris and Tom Mullen?" Madison said, annoyed.

"Just hold on," he said. "I promise this will all make sense soon enough. But you will not like it one bit."

"That seems to be the only thing type of thing I'm privy to these days."

As they followed the truck down streets of Arlington, a white van pulled out a block behind where Walter Robinson recently parked. It kept its distance from Walter's BMW but maintained a steady pace.

The driver was the man with the codename Adder.

CHAPTER 35

WALTER ROBINSON FELL BACK FROM HIS tail the further they departed from the city. The "Protect-U Shredding" truck drove to an obscure location off the main road, hidden by trees and brush. The driver made his way to a large, five-level compound with no windows surrounded by an old barbed-wire fence. The truck stopped at a guard house before a gate opened to let the truck enter the compound and drive around to the loading dock. Walter pulled his car into a clearing in the woods and turned off the engine.

Madison turned to him and said, "All right, enough is enough. What the hell is going on?"

Walter hesitated, smoothed the sleeves on his shirt, sighed and said, "I have some rather shocking things to tell you and it will be hard to hear."

"Go on."

"Fran Norris and Tom Mullen are more than colleagues. They're business partners. They are owners of 'Protect-U Shredding.' And I took a long time to find that out. Neither reported that on their financial disclosures. It's covered up by layers and layers of paperwork; corporations owning other corporations, et cetera, et cetera. And as far as I can tell they either hide the revenue from the business well or they don't take a dime which is what I think they're doing."

"Why would they do that?" Madison said skeptically.

"Because whatever they're doing in this building, it's worth more that money."

"So what are they doing in there?"

"I don't know. But that's why we're here."

"Okay, so you want to break into this private building?"

"When you put it that way it sounds kind of nefarious," Walter said, grinning.

"I'm glad you find this amusing. But there is no way I'm doing this. Forget it."

"Okay," Walter sighed again. "There is something else. Remember when Jeanne Radford told you her husband, Fran Norris and Tom Mullen were working on something big but she was not sure what it was?"

"Yeah."

"It was this. And there is another owner of 'Protect-U.' It's your father."

"What?" Madison yelled. "He's involved in all of this?"

"Maybe," Walter admitted. "William might be the fall guy. That's why I wanted you involved. We need to find out what's going on in that building. I heard Fran and Tom talking in hushed terms about the president. Those two spoke about 'taking him out' and having the ammunition to do it so their hands aren't anywhere near the crime."

Madison laughed. Walter grimaced. "Walter, they have been trying to find someone to primary him. Fran told me herself. And I already told you that. It's just politics, that's all."

Walter shook his head. "No, it's more than that."

"No, it isn't. If that's all you have then this is a big waste of time."

Walter frowned. "Madison, I don't think they're shredding anything at all in this building."

"What are you talking about?"

Walter reached in the back of his car and produced a manila folder. He handed it to Madison. "Look at this transcript from a call between Norris and Mullen. Read the highlighted part."

Madison took the folder and opened it up to pages of transcripts. On the top was a group of highlighted text that read:

Female Voice: *Have you seen the report from the latest batches?*
Male Voice: *Oh yea, and it's juicy. I think we've found what we were looking for and it's better than anything I could have imagined.*
Female Voice: *Yep [inaudible]*
Male Voice: *So do we move forward?*
Female Voice: *Absolutely. Is it time to get Madison?*
Male Voice: *Boyd killed himself to keep Madison out of this. Are you sure she's the one?*
Female Voice: *She's the only one. Boyd was wrong. Get her.*

Madison threw the entire folder in the backseat, gritted her teeth, and screamed, "Shit!" Walter just stared.

"Now you see why I brought you here. Are you ready to see what's inside?"

Madison's anger turned to determination. So many emotions swirled. The agony of Boyd's death never subsided. It had been a constant, nagging emotion in the back of her head no matter what she did. At that moment she did not care about her career, what the media might say, or if she might get arrested for breaking and entering. None of that mattered.

"Let's go," she said with as much resolve as she could muster.

Walter and Madison exited the vehicle and walked through the woods toward the back of the installation.

While Madison and Walter spoke in the car, the man with the codename Adder pulled his van toward the front of the long road that led to the "Protect-U Shredding" building. He parked under the cover of trees and brush in a perfect choke point. There was only one road leading in and out of the building. Anyone leaving would have to go past him.

Adder turned off the engine and removed his pistol. He checked the magazine and verified a bullet was in the chamber. He then secured it in its holster underneath his left arm, lit a cigarette, and waited. Adder made sure his cellphone was fully charged as he sat, ready to complete yet another mission.

CHAPTER 36

"OKAY, LET'S GO," WALTER SAID BLANKLY to Madison. They just had hid the car off a service road behind the building. Walter led Madison through the woods to a dilapidated part of the barbed-wire fence surrounding the facility. Overgrown weeds entangled the fencing. Madison followed and watched as Walter removed clippers from his pocket and went to work at the bottom of the fence. Within a few minutes he made a hole big enough for them to crawl through.

As Madison went to her hands and knees she wished she had not decided on heels and a blouse for this operation. Despite the wardrobe choice, Madison was determined to get answers. She had felt that something was rotten in D.C. Every one of her interactions with Boyd Radford, Fran Norris, and the others involved felt like it connected somehow. Madison needed to put it all together and she hoped that crawling through a security fence led to those answers.

About twenty feet separated the fence from the building. Walter crouched as he ran the length and took a knee next to what appeared to be a small window. Madison followed. She arrived as Walter wiped the grimy window with his fist and peered.

"Okay, here comes that worker we saw earlier, look."

Madison rested on her hands and knees to put her face to the glass. Inside, she saw the worker who had removed the "Protect-U Shredding" cans and placed them in the truck. The worker wheeled two cans through a locked door. After about five minutes he returned without the cans and headed back toward the entrance.

"We need to get into the building and see where he took those cans," Walter said with authority. "I think this place is—"

Before he could finish, a surly voice interrupted, "Turn around slowly and put your hands up."

Madison and Walter twisted to see two security guards with pistols in hand. A moment of panic flowed through Madison as she complied. The guards then radioed "We got them," before leading the pair to the front of the building. The guards removed Walter's gun and confiscated both of their cellphones.

They were led to the building entrance where they entered into a large room with a single security guard kiosk in the center. A tough looking man, in his fifties, but in excellent physical shape with a military swagger, casually approached the two without saying a word. He wore a security outfit and held his hands behind his back as he came face to face with Madison. Looking her up and down, he uttered "humph" then moved to Walter who shot him an evil eye. With lightning quick speed the man slapped Walter in the face with such ferocity that Walter dropped to his knees. By the time he hit the floor the security man had his hands behind his back again.

"Hey, knock it off you bastard," Madison screamed. She pushed toward the man but was promptly held back by the other guards. The security man laughed then nodded to the other guards. Two other guards appeared from an adjacent room and dragged Walter away. Madison tried to fight but they held her in a firm grasp. They picked her up, kicking and screaming, and led her toward the back of the room where an elevator waited. The guards held her in check while one of them inserted a key card into the elevator panel, punched in a numeric code, and the door closed. After the elevator dropped for what seemed like a solid five minutes, the doors opened to a nondescript hallway with a metal door waiting in the distance. Madison was escorted there where the security guards opened it to reveal a large, well-lit conference room with polished chairs and a table big enough to seat twenty people. At the back end of the room was another metal door.

The security guards pushed her into the room then backed out, shutting the door and leaving Madison alone. Madison turned and banged on the door, testing the knob and finding it locked. A sound from behind interrupted her attempt at freedom. She turned to see two figures emerging from the other metal door.

For a moment she stared in awe as they clapped in a slow, mocking, manner.

It was Fran Norris and Tom Mullen.

CHAPTER 37

"WELL DONE, MADISON," FRAN NORRIS SAID with a smile. "We are all so proud. You've come a long way since the intrepid teen eager to show the world she would not remain under the thumb of her dynastic family for long. And yes, we have been watching you the whole time."

"Well, that's creepy. What are you talking about, you freaks?" Madison practically screamed. "Why don't you let me go?"

"Soon enough," Tom Mullen said with a smile. "We have been waiting for you. The next few moments will be difficult but in the end you will see the wisdom in what we've accomplished. Would you please follow us?"

Madison scanned the room. There was no way out. She was caught and left to their mercy. Madison wanted to scream, run, and fight but it was pointless. And besides, there was something nagging in the back of her mind. She wanted to hear what they had to say. Madison had barely scratched the surface on whatever plot was being conducted inside these walls. Madison strode toward Fran and Tom as they beckoned her to walk through the back metal door. Madison's heart beat faster with every step. Her life was in danger. Of that she was sure. Walter might already be dead. And despite their cordial demeanor, Tom and Fran were too slick to let her get away to expose this operation.

In the next room beyond the metal door, Madison found herself at the top of a catwalk overlooking an expansive room filled with sounds of people below shuffling. She grabbed the rail of the catwalk and peered over the side to see about fifty people in blue, one-piece jumpsuits busy at work. The room was divided into three sections. The first section was centered by a giant hole in the wall where one of the "Protect-U Shredding" cans slid through. Without missing a beat a team of two grabbed the can and walked it over to an empty table where two others waited. Someone produced a key to unlock the can then threw back the lid. These cans were tamper-proof so no one could access anything left by clients. Confidentiality was supposed to be a mainstay of such businesses.

The team dumped the contents of the can then joined two other workers as they sorted and stacked. The workers placed all the papers into neat piles with expert efficiency and took great care to remove staples and paper clips. Each worker placed these papers face up until the can's entire contents were neatly organized.

The second section of the room contained large machines about the size of a shopping cart. On one side was a long neck-like rectangular funnel where workers placed the recently organized stacks of paper. The room was filled with sounds of whirls like a copy machine. Machines lit up and activated whenever papers were inserted. In all, there were twelve machines, each working fast. Workers waited about a minute after stacks were placed in the machines before adding another.

On the other side of the machines was the last section of the room where a dozen workers removed papers as they emerged from a funnel on the other side. The workers took the papers over to one of three oven doors in the walls at the end of the room. As they approached, the oven doors automatically opened to a small puff of smoke. Workers threw the papers into the furnace with little care.

Madison walked carefully down the catwalk, watching every step of the intricate operation. The workers in the blue jumpsuits were experts at their craft. The job was simple enough, but they did not speak and worked quickly.

"You're copying the information before you destroy it," Madison said.

"Well, more than that," Tom replied nonchalantly. "Each of these machines is a scanner. They copy everything to a hard-drive that feeds into a program the National Security Agency covertly created back in the 1980s. Back then we dealt more with documents than we do now in the digital age. But before the Internet, assets did it the hard way. They would steal documents in the dead of night, send it to a covert lab that held one of these machines, copy it to a computer, and finally replace the documents before anyone was wiser. It was horribly inefficient, and the program went unused after a short period of field testing. But of course, the government never gets rid of anything. As far as anyone is concerned these machines are still locked away in the basement of NSA headquarters at Fort Meade."

"How do you keep an operation like this covert? Who are these people?"

"It's simple," Fran interjected. "The business is run legitimately. Employees, like the one you followed to this building, drop these cans down a shoot where they assume the contents are destroyed, which they are eventually. But the employees do not understand what goes on behind these closed doors. These workers were recruited from detention centers along the southern border. All of them are illegal immigrants who were caught many times and face severe penalties and jail time. Aside from breaking into the country, they're not criminals, just people looking for work who have a lot to lose. Most don't speak or read English so they don't even realize what they're feeding into our scanners. It's a perfect relationship."

"This is madness," Madison said under her breath.

Tom huffed. "Oh, come now, Madison. Do you think this sort of thing is not done all over the world? Well, not this particular operation, but I mean covert operations completely unimaginable by the idiotic electorate?"

"So, this is a government program? For what? These documents aren't coming from a foreign government. They're coming from all over Washington, D.C. We have one of these cans on the floor where my office is located on Capitol Hill."

Tom and Fran gave each other a solemn look. They turned to Madison as Tom motioned to continue down the catwalk. Madison shook her head, seething as she headed toward another metal door at the end of the catwalk. This was more nefarious than she could have imagined. Madison opened the door to another nondescript corridor with doors along the hallway about every ten feet. How big was this complex?

Tom led her to one door, knocked, and entered. Madison followed with Fran in tow. The walls were lined with filing cabinets and a large black desk sat in the middle of the room.

Madison rolled her eyes as she saw who was leaning back in a chair behind a desk.

"Now why did I have a feeling you were involved? Hello, George."

George smiled.

CHAPTER 38

WALTER ROBINSON WANTED TO WIPE THE blood dripping from his busted lip. The guards popped him good when he refused to stop resisting as they dragged him into a small room with no windows. He sat handcuffed on an uncomfortable metal chair in the middle of the dimly lit room. His rage outweighed any notions of fear. Somewhere, Madison was in the building with God knew what happening to her and it was all his fault.

As Walter gathered his thoughts, he was interrupted by the sound of the door unlocking. A petite, black-haired, gorgeous woman in a sheer suit top and skirt entered. She had dark green eyes, and it did not take long for her exotic perfume to fill the small room. Despite her beauty, her hard face was nothing but business. The woman carried a thick folder. Walter tensed the second she made eye contact.

"You have been a busy boy," the woman said almost seductively. "We failed to realize how little respect you have for the chain of command. Your superiors have told you time and time again to drop this inquiry into Boyd Radford and now you're breaking into private property. Tsk-tsk, darling." She smiled. There is nothing worse than facing a stern woman who knows she has you cornered.

"I never much cared for authority, lady," Walter said. He spit blood on the floor, startling the woman for a moment. "And who are you?"

"Call me Simone if you like. I'm a lawyer."

"And here I believed I could not like you any less. Now, what I would like is to be out of these handcuffs. I am still an FBI agent and you have no right to detain me. A lawyer should be aware of that."

Simone giggled. "Indeed," she said throwing her head back in laughter. She opened the folder and leafed through some pages. "We have an entire dossier on you, Walter. And it is rather extensive. You failed to notify, well, anyone about this little investigation of yours. That means everything you've done today was unauthorized. Now we could go through the proper channels and file a complaint but that would bring undue attention to this company and both you and I know that can't happen."

Walter stared at the floor.

"Until now you've had a good record at the FBI," Simone continued. "A few minor incidents at the academy but nothing out of the ordinary. Now, there is a matter of your record at the Homicide Department in Omaha that could raise alarms."

Walter's eyes opened to the size of saucers. "What the hell are you talking about?"

Simone returned the stare. "Does the name 'Gerald Robinson' ring a bell?"

Walter clenched his teeth.

"Such a tragic story. Shall I remind you? An unarmed black teenager was shot and killed by a white cop in a back alley. That's a terrible way to go, don't you agree? The officer in question was pursuing someone who matched the description of a shoplifter at a nearby convenience store."

"Oh, shut up," Walter said. Spittle shot from between his teeth.

Simone glanced up for a second before returning to the folder. "The prosecutors could have nailed the cop if they had seen the body cam footage but it magically disappeared. That cop was your former partner before you were promoted to homicide. Weird, is it not?"

Walter tried to hold back his tears. "What's your bloody point, lady?"

Simone slammed the folder shut. "Let's cut this nonsense, shall we? We have more information on you than you can possibly imagine. What we do with that data is entirely up to you."

Walter did not hesitate. "I don't give a damn what you do with it."

Simone laughed again. "You might. Let me lay it out for you. This organization deals with people like you every day. You cannot imagine who we have working for us. But trust me when I say we can make your life quite hellish. So here's the deal. We are willing to forget this little incident ever happened and keep your sordid past in the past in exchange for you keeping your mouth shut about this facility. We also may call on your for a favor or a tidbit of information from time to time. That will be provided to us without delay or question."

Walter shook his head as his rage began to boil over. He almost felt like he could break the handcuffs with adrenaline.

Simone looked him up and down, held the folder to her chest, and said, "I'll give you a few moments to consider this proposal. But I will give you a piece of advice. Do not let your pride impede the right decision. After a while, you will find that our little arrangement will be lucrative as long as you show loyalty. I have seen tougher men in this situation break down over far less. Your demeanor is noble, but don't be stupid."

Simone lurched toward the door. Before she could exit Walter mocked, "So tell me, what do they have on you?"

Simone paused, holding the handle of the door for an instant. She turned and cracked a smile in the side of her mouth. "Don't be too smart for your own good."

CHAPTER 39

"YOU DO NOT UNDERSTAND HOW BIG of an operation we're running here," George said with a nefarious sneer. The deep-state operative still looked rumpled, as he always did, but more at ease than before. Madison sat in a chair opposite the desk. Fran and Tom stood behind her. "But then again, you should have some idea of how far we will go. Now don't you?"

The conversation with George back in her office flooded back. She closed her eyes and sighed.

"You told me that Shuhada' Alnnabi is a CIA front. They were created with the full backing of the U.S. intelligence service. Russia and China were never involved with them. It was all a lie."

George smiled. Fran and Tom remained silent. "I told you that to prepare you for this. We use the useful idiots in Shuhada' Alnnabi to conduct covert foreign policy. But they are only a cog in the machine. So much of what you believe controlled by the President, Congress, or some shadow agency is directed, well, out of this room. Between myself and a talented agent who does a lot of our field-work, we can get anything done anywhere in the world."

"Is this supposed to impress me?" Madison asked calmly. She was an expert at hiding her emotions. That skill was never more needed than now.

"It should," George replied. "The operation you glimpsed from the catwalk is the lifeblood of how the world works. Natural resources, military power, manpower, gold, money, and wealth are not as important as information. Information is the commodity that every nation wants, needs, and desires. Yet none of them have what we have. Every piece of paper that comes into this factory isn't just scanned; it's documented by an advanced piece of AI software. It categorizes everything and deciphers what's important, who it relates to, and places it on our servers. All we need to do is query a name, place, or event and it will pull dozens upon dozens of scanned entries. You need to not only understand our power but respect it."

Madison raised an eyebrow. She breathed slowly. "Why are you telling me all of this? What do you want from me?"

George looked up at Fran who said, "We'll get to that in a minute, dear. Everything we're telling you will make sense soon enough. What George is trying to explain is that this humble little building, and others like it, is the epicenter of the systems of power throughout the civilized world. We're not just talking about our government either. Every major nation has an embassy in DC. And most of them are as careless with sensitive documents as we are. There are those, like the Russians for instance, who destroy everything in-house. But we get enough information on their operatives from other foreign powers so we can turn them as easily. Plus, you would not believe how many people put usernames and passwords on pieces of paper."

"Absolutely," George interjected. "Take, for instance, the talented operative I previously mentioned. We discovered from a cable about a nasty little incident involving him during the second Iraq war. After we confronted the operative, he promised to do anything as long as we kept everything under wraps. It was simple. And now he's ours."

"So you are all a bunch of blackmail artists?" Madison said with a sarcastic laugh.

The room fell silent.

"I get what you're doing," Madison continued. "This is a pitch to get me to play ball. Maybe you've got some of my skeletons in your little database. I don't understand why you've targeted me and I don't care. You people are evil, corrupt, and if you don't mind, I would like to leave now, okay?"

Madison spoke so fervently that she failed to notice Fran and Tom slip out of the room. In their place, a single person quietly entered. He stood right behind her, put his hand on her shoulder, and said, "Hello, Madison."

Madison tensed and closed her eyes. She did not need to turn to see who was holding her shoulder.

It was her father.

CHAPTER 40

WALTER TRIED TO ENJOY THE MOMENTARY solitude in the dark room. His lip still dripped blood as thoughts swirled. The FBI agent had tripped into the biggest wasp's nest of his life and there were no good options for escape. Simone painted a bleak picture. Yet, since Walter's career was most likely finished, the solution became obvious.

The door creaked open. Simone glided to Walter's handcuffed position in the middle of the room and stood with arms crossed, tapping her foot. "Well?" she said impatiently.

"Okay," Walter whispered.

"Okay, what?"

"I'll play ball."

"That's what we figured," Simone said matter-of-factly. "You are a smart man. Misguided, but intelligent nonetheless."

Simone circled behind him, removed jingling keys and unlocked Walter's handcuffs. Walter rubbed his wrists before standing. He turned to Simone who stood with a defiant smirk.

Walter oozed with hatred for this woman. "So what now?"

"You will have to forgive the formality but we can't simply take your word. Before we let you go, you need to take a lie-detector test. If you pass you will go home, clean up, and go back to your normal routine." Simone led him out of the room toward the front of the building. They walked past the security kiosk where he and Madison separated earlier. The exit was twenty feet away.

Walter stopped and turned to Simone. "There is one thing though," he said with his eyes turned down facing her.

"Oh, what now?" Simone said, annoyed.

In an instant, Walter met her gaze with fire. He reared back his right hand and with one quick thrust of power, slugged the petite woman right in the face. Simone folded to the floor like clothes falling through a laundry shoot.

In the few seconds it took for security at the kiosk to realize what happened, Walter had already sprinted to the door. The last noise he heard was someone yelling, presumably on a radio, about his escape. Walter ran, ignoring pain, until he reached the hole in the fence where he had entered earlier. He crawled through, so fast he cut his hands and head on the sharp edges of the fencing. In a quick burst, he made it to his car. By the time he entered and started the vehicle the compound was swarming with half a dozen security guards, all with guns in one hand and a radio in the other.

Walter barely had his bearings when three guards opened fire in a sweeping motion from the woods behind the vehicle, ambling in a triangle. One bullet zinged through the windshield and hit the passenger side seat. Ding noises crunched as bullets entered the car at terrifying speed and precision.

"Dammit all to hell!" Walter screamed as he shifted the car into drive and slammed on the gas. He drove away from the shooters and back to the only road that led out of the compound. His car screeched as it slid onto the road. Walter pressed hard on the gas again, speeding up faster and faster.

Walter's mind raced. Yes, his career would be finished. But he could not live with himself if he did not help Madison take down whatever shadowy operation he had stumbled upon. Walter decided to head back to FBI headquarters, requisition an assault team, and be back at this compound within the hour. He hoped his bashed-in face would suffice for "probable cause" in time to catch the devilish Simone and her confederates before they disappeared.

Walter sped through the forested road and made it through unmolested as he slowed to turn on the main road and then...

BANG!

In an instant, Walter's car tumbled. His head throbbed as he lost consciousness. The side impact left the car upside down and spinning. Every window smashed as fuel and other fluids streamed from various cracks.

Walter slid in and out of consciousness in a groggy haze. Later, he woke momentarily before passing out again as someone removed him from the car and threw him into the back of a van. He thought he heard an angry Simone yelling. The things she called Walter were not fit for a men's locker room. Either Walter was delirious or her voice sounded off, almost like there was something in her mouth. Walter had almost forgotten that he slugged her. After a few minutes of driving, someone dragged Walter from the back of an empty van, handcuffed him again, and placed him in the back of a large truck.

But this one was not empty.

CHAPTER 41

GEORGE LEFT THE ROOM AS MADISON seethed. William Gladstone took a seat with his head hung low. For a moment he almost appeared humble. That partially diffused Madison's anger because, well, she had never seen her father look humble. That did not lessen his responsibility for this situation though. There was still so much she needed to learn. And those answers would come no matter what.

"Dad, you have a lot of explaining to do," Madison groaned. She squeezed the armrest of the chair with such ferocity she thought it might break off.

"I know," William said. "And I'm sorry. I really am. This was the only way."

"The only way for what?"

"To get you here. I want you involved. You're the only one smart enough, capable enough, and well, you're not just the future, Madison, you're the present. There's no one else."

Madison calmed. Damn him. Her upbringing was anything but cordial and loving. William Gladstone was always Madison's tormenter and later rival. The coldness he exhibited for so long resulted in a few nice words going a long way. Madison released her grip on the armrest but the anger did not dissipate. She took a deep breath and promised no matter what he said, she would not be manipulated. Madison eyed him, saying nothing. William appeared wounded and genuine.

"Twenty years ago," he began, "I met George. We developed a working relationship as I gave political cover to his operations. Higher powers, of course, sanctioned everything. But after a while, we both became disillusioned with the direction of the country. Politicians bluster but are afraid to do what must be done out of fear of the next election. The real work, the patriotic work, is done in the shadows. At first we did nothing unrelated to national security issues. After some time, we found that other public policy issues could be influenced just as well. Public office got in the way of this important work though. That's why I left politics behind. My effectiveness was better suited for the outside away from the cameras. Over time we determined that a vehicle to induce radical change was necessary.

"That's why we created Shuhada' Alnnabi."

"Say what?" Madison leapt out of her chair. "You are behind the most notorious terrorist organization in the world?"

"Trust me, it's all smoke and mirrors, mainly," William pleaded. "Most of the operations conducted in the Shuhada' Alnnabi name are copycats and have nothing to do with us. The attacks we've planned have purpose and attempt to minimize human casualties. But sometimes it is necessary. The world cannot change through discussion and good intentions. Only men of action have the ammunition to forge empires and sustain prosperity."

Madison paced, shaking her head. "I can't believe what I'm hearing. To what end, Dad?" She emphasized that last word. Of all the conversations between fathers and daughters, this was among the most unusual.

"The planet is dying, Maddy. I have devoted my life to environmental issues. That's no secret. But the public does not care, even faced with assured demise. If a politician talks about global warming, they're ridiculed. If you support a carbon tax, you're run out office. Half the world will be underwater in twenty years and no one wants to make hard decisions now when we can do something."

"So you know what's best for the planet and the people living in it?" Madison said shaking her head. "You sound utterly egotistical."

William raised his voice. "Ego? Are you kidding me? That's what know-nothing voters say. I want to save lives and it's all about my ego? Come on!"

"What about OPEC headquarters? Did you save lives there? Or was that another copycat?"

William said nothing. Madison winced. She felt sick to her stomach.

CHAPTER 42

ADDER SHUT THE DOOR TO THE truck with Walter placed neatly inside the back. The embattled operative turned to Simone with a grimace as she held an ice pack to her face. Her hair was disheveled, and she was as angry and as dangerous as the most gruesome killer.

"What?" she said pointedly.

"This is stupid," Adder replied, crossing his arms. "Take him in the back and put a bullet in his head. Don't toy with the man."

"It's not your job to ask questions," Simone shot back. "This is what the boss wants, and this is what will happen. Blackmail won't work with this man. Shooting him serves little purpose. This gives us cover."

Adder rolled his eyes.

"This is what I wanted to do from the beginning. We would never turn him. And what did I get for it? A shot to the face."

Adder stared lifelessly at the raging beauty.

"Do your damn job," she said turning away.

"Wait," he called out. "What about Madison?"

Simone turned and smiled.

From inside the truck, Walter tried to remain alert. The enclosure was dark and there was little room to maneuver. Lying on the ground handcuffed, he had trouble breathing and his side hurt like hell, probably as a result of broken ribs. Walter's face felt like it had gone through a meat grinder but he did his best to examine the surroundings.

The truck had no windows, and the front seats were not visible. When his eyes adjusted to the darkness he was able to make out ten large black drum barrels.

Each and every one was connected with wires.

"Oh, hell," Walter thought. He struggled to get free but every movement came with searing pain. He groaned and laid flat, his mind racing.

The voices outside the truck were faint but he picked up a few fragments.

"They need more time with Madison." he heard from what sounded like Simone. A few more muffled words then a deep man's voice said, "If you want me to make her disappear, give the order... then make sure the trail from Robinson to Shuhada' Alnnabi is as clear as possible and..." They trailed off again. Walter was not sure if it was a concussion affecting his hearing or if they were moving farther away. What the heck were they talking about? Walter was on the verge of panicking.

With as much strength as he could muster he screamed. What emitted was an incomprehensible, "UGGGHHHAAAHHHTHHHTTT!"

The voices ceased as he heard approaching footsteps. The back of the truck opened, and he came eye to eye with a tall man with what looked like a fake mustache and beard. He wore some sort of delivery man uniform. Simone stood a few feet behind him with fire in her eyes. She scowled at Walter with intense hatred.

The man in the uniform sighed and pulled out a handkerchief from his pocket and tied it around Walter's mouth. The delivery man pulled his arm back into a fist.

"Wait!" Simone yelled. The man stopped and turned around as Simone made her way to the back of the truck.

The bleeding bombshell casually pushed the man out of the way and hovered over a helpless Walter Robinson.

"You could have been a part of something important," she said angrily. Simone removed an ice pack from her face to reveal a large black welt. She tossed the solid brick of ice up and down. Then she examined Walter with a few quick glances.

"So long, Walter" she said smiling.

With a sudden force of anger-fueled strength she came down on Walter's face with the ice pack.

Everything went black again for Walter.

CHAPTER 43

"SO THE ENDS JUSTIFY THE MEANS?" Madison said with a sneer. The disdain in her voice was hard not to notice. This was a mammoth conspiracy. If the public ever learned the truth about what she discovered this morning, they would be appalled. And if what her father was saying was true, she really had no idea the things they'd been skulking about doing in the shadows for years.

William Gladstone never acted so conciliatory in his life. Some claim everyone has a soft side, or at the least a human side, but Madison had seen no evidence of that from the esteemed William Gladstone. He led his life with purpose. But the extent of that determination was only truly known by him alone. The great politician championed several causes throughout his career, with environmental policy being his biggest concern, but Madison never fathomed he would go to such lengths to see them through. The latest revelation made her wonder how far he would go with or without her involvement. And if she rebuffed him what would he do to prevent her from exposing this operation?

"We don't have time left for platitudes or politics," William said gruffly. "You've seen the reports; the planet cannot survive. There are too many people and not enough resources. My biggest fear is that we are already too late. But I can't dwell on that now. We must move forward and do what we can to save as many worthy lives as possible."

Madison took a deep breath. "So how do you expect to accomplish this? Give me specifics. What is your grand plan?"

William adjusted, sitting. "You must understand this has been in the works for years. It goes back two presidencies. A global plan is in motion to force humanity to cease their dependency on oil. And it's like tearing a drug addict away. But in this case there will be no chance for relapse because that drug will be a thing of the past." William made that statement with incredible pride.

"So you've driven up the price of oil," Madison said. "Gas is over $6 a gallon, President Wilson pushes an unrealistic energy policy and you're using your fake terrorist organization to systematically weaken the market even more. But that's not enough. What's your endgame?"

"Oil and gas will be so toxic politically and financially it will put oil companies out of business. Look, margins are not very big anyway. They put so much money into exploration and excavation that a sudden policy change will cripple the entire industry. In a year, fracking, deep-sea exploration, and even coal mining will be illegal. And you're wrong about Wilson, he will get his ambitious energy policy through Congress."

"Oh, come on, you cannot be serious," Madison said with a laugh. "No one in a competitive district will vote for such Draconian cuts to our energy industry. Besides, green technologies aren't ready to pick up that slack."

William smiled. "My organization has already secretly whipped the vote. It will be close but we've got enough of Congress in our pockets to guarantee its passage. The country will go through a few hard years for sure but the demand for solar panels, wind farms, electric cars and more will explode. And that's just the beginning of the green revolution. Vertical farming, drought-resistant crops, battery powered homes, widespread composting, and so much more will not only be embraced by this country but it will be celebrated. A few eggs to crack but the omelet will save the planet."

Madison paced again. She shook her head and cracked her knuckles repeatedly. "Is that it?" she finally said with desperation. "There's no way that will work."

"Not alone, no," William blurted. "We have contingency plans for our contingency plans. And we are thorough. It will happen. Trust me. And besides, we have another card to play that will pull all of our plans together."

"So, you've got President Wilson in your pocket?" Madison said, exasperated.

"You can say that," William smiled.

"If he gets these policies through, he's toast come election time. The president's approval ratings are already tanking. Even if you've got whoever the Republican nominee for president will be blackmailed too, there's no way he can survive without campaigning hard against what will be the most unpopular piece of legislation ever created. Dozens upon dozens of elected officials will lose reelection and never come back. All of your resources will disappear on one gambit."

William smiled even wider. "Where did you ever acquire such tremendous political instincts, Maddy? And you're exactly right. This Congress and this presidency are toast. But what we've built here is bigger than one man, woman, or congress. We read the patterns for every elected official. Everyone has skeletons, and the next elected official will be stupid enough to put something embarrassing in one of our shredding containers. Maybe that person will write down a password to an email account he uses to talk with his mistress. Or perhaps they'll trust the wrong person or try to bury something that would ruin their career. They all do it. Take this Congress and exchange every one of them for someone else, and you still have a huge stinking lot of megalomaniacs with a propensity for self-destruction."

"You think highly of yourself," Madison replied with disgust. William had barely moved a muscle during his diatribe, smiling like he held all the cards. Maybe he did. William prided himself on being unreadable. That is what made him such a formidable opponent.

"Everyone that runs for office holds some level of arrogance. Is mine any worse than anyone else you work with up on the Hill?"

He had her there. William Gladstone had a way of getting what he wanted. This operation pushed him further away from legality and into the shadows to complete his magnum opus. Now, the next few moments would be the culmination of his career for better or worse.

"Despite how you view me, I'm right when I tell you that people will forget their anger. The next president can make it look like they oppose these environmental reforms, make some half-assed attempts to repeal a few here and there, but in the end, the American people will stop paying attention and move on to something else. When the dust settles, everyone will have adapted to green energy and technology in their everyday lives. The game is all about optics, not real change. And that's when we make our final move. Yes, it all depends on who is in the White House after Lloyd Wilson."

Madison sat, crossing her legs. "That is quite a plan you've got there, Dad."

"Look, we need a leader who can complete this journey. Someone who will complete the masterplan. The person who can see this legacy I've created, take it, and run with it. That person is the leader this country has been waiting for to take them into the Promised Land, save the world, and be the president the people deserve.

"That person, Maddy, is you."

CHAPTER 44

WALTER ROBINSON AWOKE AS THE TRUCK pivoted and knocked him up against the side. He was even groggier than before, his entire body ached, and he had trouble remaining conscious. Walter could not remember ever experiencing this kind of pain. But if he did not get it together, he might not be around much longer.

Something was different: His clothes had been changed. The darkness in the truck made it impossible to decipher what he was wearing, but it was not the suit he had on before. As he lay on the floor, he scratched the ground with his head and felt tiny hairs. Someone had glued a fake beard and mustache to his face. What the heck was going on?

The truck rambled for what seemed like an hour. While it was difficult to ascertain what was happening, eventually the truck slowed to a complete stop. The truck moved a few feet, stopped again, then moved a few more feet like they were waiting in line for something. Walter almost laughed as he wondered if he was being taken through a drive-thru.

The truck stopped again and idled. Muffled voices came from the cab of the truck. Someone was having a jovial conversation. After a minute of chatting, the truck lurched forward again. Walter then had difficulty remaining still as the truck circled downward repeatedly, heading deep underground.

In a short amount of time the truck came to another stop, and the engine shut off. Walter heard footsteps approach the back and fumble with the back latch. He closed his eyes and remained motionless as the lift gate opened. Someone jumped up onto the truck bed and walked past a weak Walter. Walter cracked open an eye and identified the same man who had opened the truck lift gate prior to Simone knocking him unconscious. The driver pulled out an electrical device from his pocket and attached it to several wires emitting from the barrels. He fiddled with the device, causing it to make keypad noises like on a telephone. The man finished, set the device on the top of one barrel and then undressed.

The man removed his clothing to reveal a security guard uniform underneath his delivery uniform. He peeled off what was a fake beard and mustache and threw that, along with his clothes, on top of the barrels. Turning toward Walter, who closed his cracked open eye, the man jostled him to check if he was conscious. Walter remained unmoved. The man unlocked his handcuffs and removed the gag, placed them in his pocket, and exited the truck, closing the liftgate.

The back of the truck was illuminated softly by the electrical device the man had placed on top of the barrels. Walter labored to his feet. Wobbling, he flung himself toward the barrels and the source of the illumination. As his eyes focused on the keypad it became clearer to what he was viewing.

It was a timer. And it was counting down.

With five minutes left, Walter summoned as much energy as possible and sauntered toward the liftgate. The man who put him there must not have figured he would wake because the latch was unlocked. Walter threw open the liftgate to a flood of dim light. His head darted back and forth to discover a parking garage. There were cars everywhere but no sign of anyone. The man was long gone.

Walter screamed for help. But the garage remained silent. Wherever they were, it was in the middle of a work day. People must be busy at the offices above. Walter wanted to race out of the building but if he failed to defuse this bomb, there would be no saving whoever was here. And no one was coming to his aid.

Walter ran past a large SUV with tinted windows and glimpsed himself. Someone had changed him into the same delivery uniform that the man who had flung him in the back of the truck was wearing. He also had the same colored beard and mustache. Ripping at his face did nothing as it held tight with an epoxy or glue. Walter realized he had no time to address that now though as he headed back to the truck.

Before jumping back into the truck, he noticed a sign on a pedestal in the parking garage: "Zone C—Department of Energy."

"Oh shit."

CHAPTER 45

MADISON RECALLED SEVERAL TIMES DURING THE day where she had "reached her limit." And every time she thought nothing could shock her more than the most recent revelation. Although the conspiracy was becoming clearer, it was still too much to comprehend. As events unfolded it also became clearer in her mind what she had to do before they even made the final pitch.

Fran Norris and Tom Mullen had re-entered the room. Fran pulled up a chair and Tom circled around behind them; they both wore serious looks on their faces. Madison had not yet responded to her father's statement about pushing Madison for the White House. The art of negotiation was in full effect. And despite Madison's misgivings, she had to find a way out of this mess. That nagging thought regarding how far these people would go to get what they wanted still waded in the back of her mind.

Fran cut the tension by speaking with her best politician's voice. "Understand Maddy that most of the real power brokers in DC are sitting in this room right now. We can start or end a war. There is almost no opposition to us because people don't realize our influence. Those we have in our pockets don't know they're in our pockets. With the power we wield there is nothing we cannot accomplish. Think about that. And I mean *really* think about it, and not as a means of intimidation. What if none of the crippling politics in DC, that you hate, mattered anymore?

What if you made real reforms with a lasting impact well beyond the capabilities of a first term representative?"

Tom shuffled as he nodded in agreement. Then he turned to Madison and said, "You're the last piece of the puzzle. Lloyd Wilson knows nothing of this organization. And quite frankly, he's too damned incompetent for that type of trust. We would never give him that kind of power. But you were born for this. You must be our public face."

William Gladstone studied Madison as she listened, remaining silent, waiting to read how his daughter would react. Madison kept her best poker face as she stood, arms crossed, keeping all emotions hidden. She learned this technique from him, the master of conversational manipulation. There was a hidden battle going on in this room and a Gladstone would decide the outcome.

"I take it Peter Baylor is a part of your little operation?" Madison asked.

Tom laughed. "That little twerp? He wishes."

"Peter is just a useful idiot," Fran interjected. "There are skeletons in his closet but we have never approached him about it. That tactic is only used as a last resort. Most politicians are easy enough to squeeze through common means. Our plan needed someone like him to run for that seat and he seemed logical enough as his lust for power and influence is as much of a motivator as anything. But if we needed to pressure him toward our point of view more clearly, we could."

"Interesting," Madison replied. "And where is Walter? Is he part of your elaborate scheming?"

"Put him out of your mind," Tom said with an unexpected forcefulness. "You will never see him again."

Madison feared to inquire further as she silently panicked. What did they do to him? Was he already dead?

She had to do what she could to help him, but she was backed into a corner.

After an awkward moment of silence Madison spoke with as much relative calm given the situation. "And what of Boyd?"

Fran and Tom winced. William did not move.

"Boyd was with us," Fran said. "He helped build this organization."

"I don't believe you."

"It's true," William interrupted. "Boyd and I worked with George from the beginning. Boyd was going to be our nominee for president, but he got cold feet and you were the logical next choice. As we built an empire of information, it was he who coined what we now call ourselves."

"And what is that?"

"The inner circle."

William nodded. He still barely moved, but he was at ease. The grotesqueness of this conversation did not seem to bother him in the slightest.

"So why did he take his own life?" Madison's voice cracked. She held back her emotion, remembering Boyd's smiling face, his loving wife Jeanne, and the flood of memories stemming back to her childhood.

"Boyd was a conflicted man," William replied compassionately. "I loved him like a brother. As we grew bigger and made bolder moves, he lost his nerve. When we activated Shuhada' Alnnabi and pushed for your involvement, he broke down. There is no doubt I feel responsible for his death and we all mourn his loss. But Boyd was wrong about a lot of things. You are the key to all of this, Madison, there's no one else who can do it. Democrats will follow you because you're a Democrat. Your moderate stances will siphon off enough Republican and Independent voters.

And we can pull strings to discredit your competition and put you in the White House.

"Are you willing to join the team or not?"

CHAPTER 46

TEARS FELL FROM WALTER ROBINSON'S FACE. The timer on the bomb was under a minute. The level of stress, frustration, and anger overshadowed his physical pain. He could barely move but his level of adrenaline might give him a fighting chance to escape. Walter had never been in this building before and had no idea if there was a safe way out. But could he live with himself if he ran?

Guilt invaded every fiber of his body and mind as he put away thoughts of running and focused on a complex system of wires on the triggering device. Walter had no training in bomb defusal and no one with that knowledge was coming to help. If he pulled the wrong wire, then the whole thing might explode. And the man who put him in this position took his handcuffs off and left the liftgate unlocked. He clearly was not worried that Walter would wake up and try to stop this bomb.

And that disturbing thought invaded his mind like a cavalry charge.

So that left Walter with two choices as the timer hit forty-five seconds and counting: frantically pull wires or get the hell out of there.

And as the seconds counted down, it was time to make a decision that may or may not cost hundreds, perhaps thousands of lives.

CHAPTER 47

MADISON ANGUISHED. IT WAS BECOMING INCREASINGLY difficult to keep her composure. The battle in this little room
underneath an ocean of formidably damaging information
waged. What she said and did next would reverberate in
the power structures of the world. She had to be careful.

"There is no doubt in my mind," she began, "that what
you're doing is wrong."

Fran surprisingly nodded in response. Tom and
William remained like statues. "However," she continued,
"part of me hates to admit it but Washington is crippled by
indecision and political maneuvering. In a perverted way,
I can see why you are doing what you're doing, even if I
disagree with the method. But if I was with you, and I'm
not saying I am, how is anyone supposed to beat an incumbent president—even one as unpopular as Wilson?"

"As I said," William Gladstone said with nonchalance,
"we flourish by being thorough. Wilson will resign."

"How can you predict that?"

William raised an eyebrow. "You will see soon enough."

Madison raised an eyebrow of her own.

"We don't want you bogged down in the details, and
instead focus on campaigning for president. The rest of the
work will go on behind the scenes. And, Maddy, I will be
there to endorse you when you formally announce your
intention to run."

Madison almost smacked herself. That should have
meant nothing. It was her father trying to throw her a bone.

She hated herself for it, but that offer, no matter how phony it was, meant something to her deep inside. *Dammit.*

"Wilson will take all the political flack and you will avoid being dragged down with him," William said. "He will get our environmental initiatives through and then get crucified. His presidency will go from toxic to radioactive. When he resigns that will lead to a power vacuum. The vice-president will take his place but he's too old and has no desire to run for a full term himself. He will announce that he will leave office when he's done filling out Wilson's term. By the time you're in the White House the worst will be over. You'll be free to keep these policies in place and move on to the next steps."

"So, you mean for me to be a puppet?"

"No, Maddy, of course not. We simply want to save the planet. You can be the president you want to be and change the world for the better. We are all aware that you have a good heart. And by the look on your face I can tell you see this method of ours as distasteful and wrong. I lay awake at night from the horrible things we've done. Do not think of me as an inhumane monster. This is not how I wanted it to go. But we're at a crossroads and if we don't act now, it will be too late. The ends *do* justify the means.

"Take the deal. Become our champion. And be the greatest leader this world has ever known. We want you to lead us. And I'll be the first person to get behind you. It's up to you, Maddy."

CHAPTER 48

FIGHT OR FLIGHT.

Those words rang in Walter's ears. Should he fight? Fight for the lives of the employees in the Department of Energy. Employees with families. They sat upstairs trying to better this country. They did not deserve a death sentence. If he fought, then their names would not be emblazoned on a memorial wall somewhere. Maybe they would do great things for themselves and this country. Or perhaps they would waste their lives. Either way, they would at least have the opportunity.

"Flight" also loomed large in Walter's mind. Chances were, defusing this bomb was impossible. If he pulled out wires, he would probably set the bomb off. He had no doubt the authorities would blame him for this horrific crime. The people that did this would make sure of that. His name would become synonymous with Osama bin Laden and Timothy McVeigh. It would all be a lie but that would not matter. But he would be alive. Fighting back against the monsters who perpetrated this crime would be possible. The FBI would no longer be in his future. But he would wreak havoc on those responsible with a vengeful fury.

The seconds counted down... 45... 44... 43. Walter continued to cry and sweat.

It was now or never.

Hero or zero.

Fight or flight.

...

With the clock of inescapable doom counting down, Walter made a life-altering decision.

...

He ran.

He sprinted toward the nearest exit as fast as his broken body would allow.

...

From that day forward, the explosion at the Department of Energy was compared with the worst terrorist attacks in the history of the world.

Hundreds of employees' lives were snuffed out in an instant. Others took days to die within the rubble as emergency crews failed to desperately pull them to safety.

Also killed were individuals whose deaths would demolish the last remnants of a sane oil and gas market. The secretary of energy was in the middle of a meeting with the last remaining players in OPEC, along with the Venezuelan and Saudi ambassadors.

If they had lived, they would have announced a new path forward in oil and gas exploration that would have stabilized the markets. A monumental deal made behind the back of President Wilson.

Instead, the energy sector faced an uncertain and dangerous future.

CHAPTER 49

"MADDY, WE'VE LAID IT ALL OUT for you. We can change the world, together. Are you with us? Will you be the leader this country needs and deserves?"

"This is what you were born for," Fran said with a smile. "We can change the world. No, we can *save* the world."

"The planet is calling you," Tom added. "So, what will it be?"

"Yes, Maddy, what will it be?" William said.

Madison hesitated. What she said next would change the course of history. And in that moment it all became clear. She had to do something unexpected. Madison needed to make the decision these people, these blackmailers, terrorists, and murderers never saw coming.

It was all too obvious. And yet, so very difficult.

"Yes," Madison said with an incredible amount of authority in her voice. "I will be your president."

EPILOGUE

"SO, YOU RECENTLY ANNOUNCED A WORLD tour." Reginald Goldsmith wore his finest suit. He had prepared well for the interview that might be the most important moment of his career. Sitting across from him in-studio was the pop sensation Bailee. "And you have said it will be the biggest and most glamorous set of shows in your career. Is that so?"

Bailee wore a black sequined dress that sparkled in the lights of the studio. Her brownish-red curly hair flowed like a cape. Bailee was fresh off a commanding performance on *Saturday Night Live* and the release of her latest album was already smashing records. She had the look of the most dominant female vocalist in the world, which came natural to her, because she was.

"Absolutely. I am so proud of everyone who took part planning this tour. Not only will it showcase my latest album but it will spread a message of love and hope that will resonate with the world."

Reginald grimaced. "That's lovely. Now, it would be irresponsible of me to not ask you about all of your recent political activism. You have caused quite a stir lately."

"Okay."

"You're a staunch supporter of President Wilson and you've gotten behind his recent environmental reforms which at first were met with scrutiny and ridicule. But he shocked the world and pushed groundbreaking measures through Congress. There is no doubt the public is not happy with him or any elected official at the moment. Do you regret taking such a stance for an unpopular position?"

"Oh, not a chance!" Bailee said emphatically. She sat back in her chair and crossed her legs. "The president is a true leader. He knows what's best for this country and is not afraid to take on unpopular positions. And my music really jives with that. Everyone should have a voice and be unafraid to make hard choices no matter what the consequences."

Reginald perked up. "Is that so?"

"Indeed."

"You have a tremendous amount of loyalty to President Wilson. A man who has approval ratings dipping into the twenties."

"Well, that sort of thing doesn't matter to me."

Reginald adjusted his glasses and sat straighter. He gave Bailee a half-smile. "Now you and the president are close, aren't you?"

Bailee hesitated then cleared her throat. "I would not say that. I admire the man for sure and I've done a few fundraisers for his causes. Occasionally, we have spoken. I would consider him a friend but we…"

"Did you sleep with him?" Reginald cut in. Bailee was stunned. Her eyes widened, and she almost jumped out of her seat.

"What? That's outrageous. How dare you!"

"Bailee, tomorrow morning a certain investigative journalist for *Vanity Fair* will publish a detailed report on a liaison you allegedly had with President Wilson in the White House. The author of that report has eyewitness accounts and documents showing you secretly spent the night at the White House while the First Lady was on vacation in Spain with her and the president's two daughters."

"I... uh... Now wait a damn minute!"

"Furthermore," Reginald picked up a paper from his desk and read, "This report, which was given to us exclusively prior to its publication, says there is a tape of a conversation between you and the president that describes some rather tawdry details."

"You are disgusting!" Bailee shouted as she fumbled to pull off her microphone attached to her dress. "This is garbage. I won't be a part of this!"

Bailee stood to walk off stage.

"Bailee, please, there is one more thing. Please." Reginald motioned for her to sit down.

Bailee stopped. Her face tensed. Her arms were like claws. But she sat down, gently.

"This report makes one more startling allegation."

Bailee blinked. But did not move a muscle. Fear oozed from her eyes. She began to sweat.

"The author claims you're pregnant."

"Oh, God," Bailee gagged. Her head almost hit the table as she broke down sobbing. She struggled to breathe. The sobs grew louder.

"Please, please," Reginald patted her back. "It's okay. This would have come out sooner or later. But you can still make this right."

Bailee continued to weep.

"It's time to come clean, Bailee. The world deserves the truth. Tell me. Is Wilson or your husband Kronik the father of your unborn baby?"

Bailee sobbed even more. Her mascara dripped from her face like a waterfall. She wrapped her arms around her head. She couldn't move, paralyzed with fear. Finally, she sniffed and wiped her nose from under her wall of arms.

And in a muffled voice she replied, "God forgive me. I... am... not... sure."

Back in his home in Stanley, Virginia, William Gladstone turned off the Newscycle with Reginald Goldsmith. He retreated to his bar and poured himself a tall glass of Wasmund's Single Malt.

"There's no turning back now," he said with a smile.

Then, he laughed.

CPSIA information can be obtained
at www.ICGtesting.com
Printed in the USA
LVHW041225170723
752371LV00005B/926